"A debut that is equal par[...]
when you're talking a[...]
a chance to be to Vegas w[...]

—Tod Goldberg, author of *Living Dead Girl*

———

"Funny and engaging. I cared about
every single character. It's a great read."

—Al Bernstein, ESPN Sportscaster

———

"If you'd tried telling me that someone could successfully blend
the hard-nosed old Las Vegas with new-age energies and
an appropriately karmic ending, I wouldn't have
believed you, but Rouff has pulled it off."

—Andrew N.S. Glazer, gambling columnist,
Detroit Free Press, and author of *Casino Gambling the Smart Way*

———

"A page-turner of a novel, with some kick to the plot and great
characters, as well as thrilling crap action."

—Frank Scoblete, #1 best-selling gaming writer in America

———

"The characters are so lifelike, the dialogue is almost like eaves-
dropping on real conversations."

—Barney Vinson, author of *The Vegas Kid*

———

"Rouff's language is uncluttered, his plot strong, and his vision
lucid. The final key to his success is a comic essential that
doubles as a superb narrative tool: a faultless sense of timing."

—John Ziebell, *Las Vegas Mercury*

———

"I enjoyed reading *Dice Angel* on the flight to Vegas
more than joining the Mile High Club."

—Steve Schrette, publisher of the
Everything Las Vegas newsletter

Dice Angel

Dice Angel

by
Brian Rouff

Hardway Press
Las Vegas, Nevada

Dice Angel

ISBN: 0-9717148-1-9

Cover Design: Alex Raffi
Interior Design and Production: Laurie Shaw

1st Printing: January 2002
2nd Printing: March 2002
3rd Printing: June 2002
4th Printing: November 2002
5th Printing: July 2003

This story is a work of fiction. Any resemblance to individuals living or dead is purely coincidental.

Hardway Press is an imprint of 21st-Century Publishing

Dedication

For Ruth and Morris

Acknowledgements

When I started compiling this list of people who helped along the way, I realized what a lucky guy I am.

To my first readers: D.J. Allen, my virtual son. Thanks especially for the graphic description of our local morgue. W. Scott Brown, who's even more cynical than I am (a compliment, by the way). Bob Burris, my oldest friend and the funniest man on the planet. Kurt Lehman, for the detailed notes and keen insight. I hope I can return the favor soon. And my long-time mentor, Larry Wilde, for his encouragement, on-target advice, and generosity of spirit.

To Deke Castleman, genius editor and friend, who "gets it." Who else would count the "dee-da-dee's"?

To graphic artist extraordinaire Alex Raffi, for the cool cover design. And to author Michael Silverhawk, for showing me a better way.

To Marianne Hill, for the primer on hypnotic regression.

To my niece, Sydney Badendyck, for the wonderful true-life material.

To my sister, Trudy Altman, my biggest fan and supporter.

To my daughters, Emmy and Amanda, who always believed in me.

And to Tammy, my wife, partner, and best friend, for her honesty, patience, and unflagging optimism. I couldn't have gotten to the finish line without you.

1

The ringing phone ripped through my sleep like a buzz saw. I caught it on the fourth ring, nearly knocking the lamp off the end table in the process. Squinting through bleary eyes, I could barely make out the time. 3:11 a.m. "This can't be good," I muttered out loud, even though I was alone. Hoping for a wrong number I barked, "What?"

"James Delaney, Jr.?" an official-sounding voice asked. The little hairs stood up on the back of my neck.

"Who wants to know?"

"Officer Robert Ramos, Metro Police, sir."

For a brief horrible moment, I pictured my seven-year-old daughter Jenny, dead in the gutter. But that was impossible. Jenny was in Salt Lake with my ex-wife Joy. And Salt Lake, as far as I know, outlawed gutters years ago.

Trying to sound casual despite my heart beating double-time, I asked, "What can I do for you, Officer?"

"They hit your place again."

"Shit! I'm on my way."

In the time it would take to ask more questions, I could be there. Wide awake now, I threw on a pair of faded jeans and a UNLV sweatshirt as I fumbled for my keys, a million thoughts racing through my mind. How the hell could they have gotten past my new super-high-tech security system? Maybe it's true what the cops say, that locks and alarms only keep out honest people. And honest people are in short supply here in Vegas, or anywhere else for that matter.

I took the steps two at a time. As I flung open the front door, a blast of cold night air hit me in the face, sending an involuntary shudder through my body. Even after more than twenty years in the godforsaken desert, I'm still surprised by the extreme temperatures. Too fucking hot in the summer, too goddamned cold in the winter. Probably a lot like living on the moon, except for the gambling.

Jumping into my '97 Mazda 626, the last sensible remnant of my married days, I peeled out of the driveway and headed for my bar. The screeching noise would most likely jar a neighbor or two out of a restful night's sleep. Good, I thought with grim satisfaction. Why should I be the only one up on a night like this?

2

It's a ten-minute drive from my condo to Jimmy D's, the saloon and supper club that bears my name. I made it in five. Ordinarily, I like driving at night, especially on those rare occasions when I have the road to myself. Sometimes I even play slalom with the orange traffic cones that line most Vegas streets these days, the cones that locals refer to as the official state bush. But tonight, speed was my only concern. Not only to find out what the hell was going on, but to outrace the dark thoughts bubbling just below the surface of my brain. If this was an isolated incident, I could handle it. But it was starting to feel like the beginning of another long losing streak. Well ... that was something better left alone for now.

Squealing into the nearly deserted shopping center parking lot, I aimed the car toward the familiar corner slot, where Jimmy D's sits nestled between a bakery and a travel agency. When my father, the original Jimmy D, uprooted my brother and me and trekked across the country more than two decades ago, the bar's location at West Sahara and Jones was at the far edge of Las Vegas. I can remember gazing westward and seeing nothing but sand and tumbleweeds. It reminded me of a scene out of some old cowboy movie. Most people, including the rest of the family, thought the old man was crazy. Nobody would drive all the way out there for a beer and a pizza. But Vegas locals were soon drawn to the friendly Irishman and word got out that his Detroit-style pizza was bigger and better than anything the Italians or the chain restaurants had to offer.

It seemed like everybody loved Jimmy D's. Everybody but me, an eighteen-year-old kid who felt like an outcast in this desolate wasteland, forced to finish my senior year of high school among strangers, resenting every minute I had to help Pop at his stupid joint. But, the place got under my skin. After awhile, I was helping out behind the bar, grilling up the burgers when the cook called in sick, glad-handing and swapping stories with the regular clientele. As Jimmy Sr. said proudly on more than one occasion, "The apple doesn't fall very far from the tree."

Over the years, Las Vegas grew up around our popular little watering hole, enveloping it like a neon cocoon, so that it's now pretty much in the center of town. By the time Jimmy Sr. died of a heart attack in 1993, Jimmy D's was a local institution, consistently topping the readers' surveys in the Vegas newspapers. More than five hundred customers turned out for the funeral, an odd assortment that included everyone from borderline street people and political hotshots to a smattering of casino moguls. It was a moving testament to the old man's life. The bar, I suddenly realized, was my father's legacy. I vowed, then and there, to continue the tradition.

One refurbishing, two expansions, and three break-ins later, I swung into a parking space next to the only other vehicle, a shiny new Metro squad car. Briefly surveying the tavern's exterior, I was relieved to see the windows intact. Whatever had happened, this wasn't your garden-variety smash-and-grab. A uniformed officer met me at the door.

"I'm Delaney," I said, extending my hand. Christ, the cop looked like a teenager. Well, who the hell else were they gonna put on the graveyard shift?

"Officer Robert Ramos," the cop said, giving my hand a perfunctory squeeze. "We spoke on the phone."

"Where's the Z-man?" I asked.

"Who?"

"Officer Zelasko."

"Oh, you mean *Sergeant* Zelasko. He got kicked upstairs. He's a desk jockey now. Why, you know him?"

"We went to high school together. I'll have to be sure to call and congratulate him on the promotion."

"Maybe you better not. I hear he isn't too happy about it."

"All the more reason," I said with a slight grin. "So what's it look like in there?"

"See for yourself."

Expecting the worst, I stepped through the door. At first glance, everything appeared to be in order. Big-screen TV in one piece, guitars and keyboard still set up in the small lounge area, Detroit Tigers memorabilia still covering the walls, including my prized Al Kaline autographed jersey.

"I don't get it," I said.

"Come with me."

I followed Ramos to the oversized bar, a gleaming mahogany and brass artifact, circa 1870, that my father brought down from a condemned Virginia City hotel.

Only then did I notice the fifteen bartop video poker machines. Each one had been carefully pried open and emptied of its contents.

"Shit," I said under my breath. "They must've gotten away with over twelve grand."

"Whoever did this really knew what they were doing," Ramos said.

"They certainly took their time. How'd they get in?"

Ramos' eyes went to the false ceiling, where one entire section of acoustical squares had been meticulously removed. The hole it left was just big enough for a man.

"They broke into the bakery through the back door, then climbed into the crawl space above the stores, and the rest, as they say, is history."

"I never liked history," I said. "Well, at least they didn't trash the place like those kids did last time."

"I don't think this was kids. Employees, maybe. Looks like it could be an inside job."

I couldn't help saying, "Inside job, huh? Where'd they teach you to talk like that, the Academy?" Ramos ignored the comment.

I continued, "I don't think any of my people would have done this. They've all been with me too long. They're like family."

"If you ask me, you can't trust anybody these days. Even family."

Nobody asked you, I thought, but decided to hold my tongue for once. Instead, I said, "I guess I should have bought a fucking alarm for every store in the center."

"We have a saying on the force. 'Alarms only keep out …'"

I cut him off. "I know, I know. Honest people."

Ramos started to get a little peeved about me short-circuiting his routine. "Well, it's true," he said petulantly.

"I don't suppose you got any prints."

"You suppose right."

"So what are the chances you'll find these guys?"

Ramos shook his head. "We'll keep an eye out for your dollar tokens at all the local joints. But, unless you're willing to let us interrogate the help …"

"Forget it," I said.

"Then, to be honest with you, the chances are slim and none. And slim just …"

"Don't tell me. Left town."

"Yeah."

"You know what I think?" I asked.

"What?"

"I think you could use some new material."

3

"What do you mean I'm not covered?" I asked, snapping a pencil in two. I was sitting behind the beat-up desk in my cramped telephone booth of an office, talking to Barry Simpkins, a poor excuse for an insurance agent. Simpkins—a large man, early forties, with an unruly shock of blonde hair and the worst case of adult acne I've ever seen. It settled in around his nose, making his honker look like a hundred-watt bulb in the middle of an otherwise bland face. You'd think, with all the money I'd given him over the years, he'd go see a dermatologist.

"Please lower your voice," Simpkins said. "I won't talk to you if you're going to scream at me."

"Promise?" I said, still a little too loudly. It was only the middle of this increasingly miserable day. I'd already spent an aggravating morning on the phone with the assholes from Gaming Control, then tried to track down the crook from the alarm company, only to discover that the place was out of business. I couldn't even hear myself think, with the work crew just outside my office door, banging away at the bartop slots.

As if reading my mind, Simpkins asked, "Do they have to make that racket?"

"They do if they're gonna get the damned things fixed in time for the Friday night rush," I said.

Simpkins rustled some papers. "Well, as I was telling you," he shouted over the ruckus, "your policy insures losses from slot theft or burglary up to two thousand dollars. Unfortunately, you're responsible for the balance. See, it says right here on page three under section D, paragraph twenty-one." He indicated some tiny print on a document that looked like hieroglyphics to me.

"Save it!" I shouted back. "The only thing I want to know is, how could you sell me such a piss-poor policy?"

Simpkins looked genuinely hurt. "Now Jimmy, you told me to keep the premiums low because your ex-wife was killing you with alimony and child support-payments. You remember that, don't you?"

He had me there. "Yeah, I guess so. Just get me the stinkin' two grand and we'll call it square."

"I can have it to you in less than seventy-two hours."

"Swell."

"You know, we could attach a rider to the policy that will cover all losses in the event that you suffer the same kind of ..."

"Barry," I interrupted. "Stuff the sales pitch."

"If you say so."

"I say so. And Barry."

"Yes?"

"On your way out, tell those guys they better not be taking another break."

After Simpkins left, I made a half-hearted attempt at organizing my desk, gave up, and decided to head for home. I was beat. Maybe I could catch a nap before happy hour.

"Keep an eye on things," I told Bev, the day-shift manager I inherited from my father. A skinny woman in her early sixties, Bev lives entirely on coffee and cigarettes, as far as I can tell. In all the time I've known her, I've never seen her eat a complete meal. Or even a snack, for that matter. It's especially strange because she manages a restaurant. Hell, she could eat for free. But she outworks women half her age and I kind of like having her around, even when she mouths off to me in front of the other employees.

"You're a real pisser," I tell her at those times, and she laughs that raspy smoker's laugh that suddenly turns into a coughing fit. "I'm gonna quit these goddamn things someday," she'll say for the umpteenth time. "They're too expensive."

Now though, she said, "You okay, hon?"

"Yeah, Bev, I'm fine. I just have to get outta here for awhile."

"You do that," she said. "Don't worry about a thing."

"I won't. We've been through tougher times than this."

She sort of cocked her head, gave me a funny look, and said, "You know, your father'd be proud of you."

"That means a lot to me," I said, giving her a quick kiss on the cheek. Her backhanded swat just missed tattooing my ass.

"You're losing your timing," I laughed as I headed out the door.

By the time I made it back to the condo, it was 2:45. Almost twelve hours since the phone call. As usual, I tried to ignore the flashing red light on the answering machine and crawl straight into bed, but I never can leave the blasted thing alone. The quivering digital voice, a cross between a drowning man and HAL from *2001: A Space Odyssey*, informed me I had two messages.

The first message was from my ex-wife. Joy. A misnomer if there ever was one. It's like she's spent her entire life rebelling against that name. Instantly, I felt myself freeze up. She never calls unless she wants something.

"Jimmy, it's Joy," she began, as if I could ever mistake that shrill whiny voice. It has all the charm of a dentist's drill. Early in our so-called relationship, before I fell out of lust, it barely fazed me. Amazing what a man will overlook for spectacular sex. Only after the divorce did every single one of my friends have the nerve to say, "How could you stand that voice? If I was married to her, I'd have to donate my ear drums." Some friends.

She droned on, "I need you to take Jenny this weekend. I know it's not your turn, but something's come up. Call me." Click. Wasn't that just like her? Not a "please" in sight.

Ignoring the ex-Mrs. Delaney, I reached for a piece of nicotine gum and jammed it into my mouth. I quit smoking last year, and now I'm addicted to the gum. When the cravings get really bad, I stick on a patch. I haven't tried chewing the patch yet.

I pushed the button again and played the second message. "Hey, buddy," growled the familiar baritone of Walter "Wally" Zelasko, recently promoted to Sergeant. "I heard what happened last night. I'm stopping by the bar after my shift. You're buying."

Same old Wally. Despite the fact he's a first-class mooch, he's also my best friend. Even though we don't talk all that often, we always pick up right where we left off. Usually with a barrage of insults straight out of high-school gym class.

A quick nap and a long shower brought me back to life. By the time I returned to the bar, I was feeling almost human. And entering the bar returned me the rest of the way to normal. After all these years, I still get a charge out of walking through the front door. It's probably similar to an actor who gets an adrenaline rush before going on stage. In a way, I'm acting too: "Jimmy D, Congenial Host." You won't see any Oscars on my mantle, but it's the part I was born to play.

The place was busier than usual for a Wednesday. Like the planets lining up just right, three factors came together to pack the joint: the Runnin' Rebels were on the tube, the fifteenth of the month was payday for many of my regulars, and it was "All You Can Eat Corned Beef and Cabbage Night." It did my heart good to see the bar jammed with patrons only too happy to refill my video poker machines, which seemed to be back in working order. It was even more crowded in the dining room, where every table was occupied and small groups waited for their names to be called as soon as dirty dishes could be whisked away. With a well-practiced eye, I scanned the room for babes. Not much happening in that department. A definite C-minus.

"Good numbers," I said to Bev. "Everybody show up for work tonight?"

"Yes, thank God. Although that new gal, Brandi, isn't catching on as fast as I'd like. She can't tell the difference between ranch dressing and blue cheese."

"Tell her the blue cheese has bigger chunks and smells like shit."

"Nice," Bev said, wrinkling her nose. "That oughta do the trick."

"Well, it's time to work the room. My public awaits."

Like a politician running for re-election, I wound my way through the bar, stopping now and then to pump a few hands, clap a few backs, kiss a few babies.

"Evening, Your Excellency," I said to the honorable Thomas Evans, Municipal Court judge. With his walrus mustache and ten-gallon hat, he looked like an older version of the Marlboro Man.

"Jimmy, good to see you!" he yelled over the din of the crowd. "It's a shame about your machines. If those hooligans ever have the misfortune of showing up in my court room, I'll throw the book at them."

"Damn right," I said, getting into the spirit of things. "Lock 'em up and throw away the key."

In the restaurant, I paused to say hi to Harvey Campbell, the Dean of Southern Nevada Community College, enjoying a pepperoni pizza with the missus.

"Everything okay, folks?" I asked.

"Always," Harvey said in his syrupy Southern drawl. "Sit down, Jimmy. Take a load off."

"Just for a second," I said. He scooted over to one end of the booth and I scrunched in. "Mrs. Campbell, nice to see you again," I said, shaking her hand. "Harve, I'd still like to know how you got such a good-looking wife."

"I have no earthly idea," he said with a shrug. "You'll have to ask her that."

"Well?"

She smiled. "I think it had something to do with copious amounts of alcohol."

"That explains a lot," I said. "You ever sober up and decide to leave this guy, give me a call. I'll keep you in chicken wings and fries for the rest of your life."

"That's hard to resist," she said with a shake of her head.

"You hear any good jokes lately?" Harvey asked.

"Only one I can tell in mixed company. Three dogs are sitting in the vet's office. The first dog says to the second dog, 'What are you here for?' The second dog says, 'Well, when the mailman came up the walk the other day, I couldn't help myself and I bit him. My owner's having me put to sleep.' 'Bummer,' the first dog says. Then the second dog asks, 'What are you here for?' The first dog says, 'The little girl next door is always teasing me, pulling my tail and stuff. Yesterday, I couldn't take it any more, so I bit her. My owner's putting me to sleep too.' The second dog says, 'Bummer.' Then

they both look at the third dog and ask, 'So what are you here for?'
And the third dog says, 'The other night my owner was getting
out of the shower. When she was bending over, I couldn't help
myself, so I mounted her.' The second dog says, 'Oh, so you're
here to be put to sleep, too.' "Nah,' says the third dog. 'I'm getting
my nails trimmed.'"

"Thanks for cleaning it up," Harvey said between laughs.

"A classic," Mrs. Campbell said.

I stood up. " Well, folks, I've got to get back to work. It's always a pleasure."

"Same here," Harvey said.

Before I got too far, Bev stopped me. "Phone's for you," she
said. "It's your ex."

"Tell her I'm not here."

"Too late. She wouldn't believe me, anyway."

"Remind me to fire you." I took the phone and cradled it between my ear and shoulder. "Jimmy D," I said, pretending not to
know who was on the other end.

"Cut the crap, Jimmy," said Joy. "How come you never return
my calls?"

"I've had a tough day. You were like last on my list of priori-
ties. Maybe even lower."

"Do you think we could have an adult discussion?" she asked
impatiently. "Just once?"

"Probably not."

"Well, write this down. I'm putting Jenny on a plane Friday
night. Southwest flight eighteen oh one. It arrives at seven fifteen.
You'll need to watch her all weekend."

"Well, since you asked so nice. What's the big deal, anyway?"

She paused briefly before saying, "I'm getting married."

Despite all we'd been through, or maybe because of it, I was
blindsided by a twinge of regret, possibly even a pang of jealousy.
Thankfully, it was followed by a tiny burst of delight, something I
hadn't experienced for a very long time.

"Congratulations," I said, sounding more sincere than I'd intended.

"Thanks, Jimmy." For once, she sounded real, too. "But you
still have to pay child support."

"Gladly. So who's the lucky guy?"

"Roger Young."

"Of the Salt Lake City Young's?"

"Ha ha. If you must know, he's a distant relative of Brigham."

"Aren't they all?"

"You're such a racist."

"Technically, I'm a bigot. So what's this Roger Young do for a living? Oil tycoon? Cyber billionaire? Prince?"

"He's a fire fighter."

That one caught me off guard. "You're shitting me. A fireman? How the hell are you going to live on a fireman's salary?"

"I'm not like that any more," Joy said quietly.

"Since when?"

"Since I found out what real love is."

Ouch. "So, when's the wedding?"

"We haven't set a date yet. He's taking me down to Panguitch to meet his parents."

"Why can't Jenny go?"

Another pause. "We don't want to complicate things right now."

"Translation: They don't know you have a kid."

"Just butt out, Jimmy. It's none of your business, anyway."

"It is where my daughter's concerned. Listen, I get to meet Mr. Right before you tie the knot. Got that?"

"I'll think about it. So are you picking up Jenny or aren't you?"

"Of course I am."

"Just make sure you don't keep her hanging around the bar all weekend. All that smoke and noise isn't good for her."

"She loves the bar," I said flatly; we'd been through this a thousand times. "Besides, I'm short-handed."

"Nothing's changed with you, I see."

"Okay, I'll take her to a movie or something."

"G-rated."

"Scout's honor."

"You were never a scout."

"Show's what you know. I was too a scout."

"Oh yeah? For how long?"

"Two weeks."

"Two whole weeks," she repeated. "You never told me that. What happened?"

"We went on a camping trip and a bear got into our food. They made us eat bark and leaves."

"So you quit."

"Actually, they kicked me out. I'd smuggled in some candy bars and potato chips."

"I hope you shared with the other kids."

"Sort of."

"What's that supposed to mean?"

"I sold it to them. Made almost fifty bucks."

"You're a real piece of work, Jimmy, you know that?"

I knew better than to tell her I took that as a compliment.

4

There's an old joke that goes, "Why is divorce so expensive? Because it's worth it." The whole five years I was married to Joy, we only had one argument. It started the minute I said "I do," and ended, more or less, when I signed the final papers. It was always about the same thing: money. Our last fight was pretty much like all the others.

"The American Express bill came today," I said, when she came home one night after going out to dinner with the girls.

"So?" she answered, daring me to go on. Funny how a two-letter word can drip with so much disdain.

"So," I repeated, trying to keep my cool, "it's over four grand. Again. That's more than the mortgage, the day care, and all the utilities combined."

"I needed some things. Jenny needed some things, too."

Playing the Jenny card already. That was low. "Look at this," I said, pointing to the statement. "Two hundred seventy-eight dollars for a purse."

"It's a Coach," she said, as if that explained anything.

"I don't care if it came with the whole goddamned team!" I shouted. I could feel my blood pressure ratchet up a couple of notches.

"Besides," Joy said, "we can afford it."

"Says who? I don't know where you got the idea that the bar is your own personal ATM machine."

"I see all the money you take in."

"Yeah, but I don't see you looking over my shoulder while I pay the bills! You ever heard of expenses? Why do you think I work eighty hours a week?"

"That's another thing," she said, and I knew exactly what was coming. "You don't spend enough time with the family."

"Jesus Christ, are you nuts? You want to know why you're able to buy all this shit? Because I work my ass off, that's why." I paused for effect. "You know what I think?"

Joy stuck out her chin and said, "I'm sure you're going to tell me."

"Damn right I am. I think you're a shopaholic, or whatever they call people like you. Mall junkies, maybe."

"You're wrong. I can stop any time I want."

"Then stop, please!"

"I don't want to."

"You need professional help. Shopper's Anonymous. What's the deal with all these appliances, anyway? A food processor, a bread machine, a créme brulè torch, for God's sake. You don't even fucking cook! You're killing me, that's what you're doing."

"Don't be so dramatic."

"It's the truth. I went into that little taco shop for lunch today and you know what happened? The kid undercharges me a dollar. I look at the receipt and he's giving me the senior discount. The senior fucking discount! I'm not even forty yet!"

"How old was the kid? Eighteen, nineteen? All adults look like seniors to him."

"Bullshit. See these bags under my eyes? These worry lines? They're all your fault."

"Just tell me one thing," Joy said. "Did you take the discount?"

"What's that got to do with anything?"

"Answer the question. Did you take the discount?"

"Of course I did."

"You're such a cheapskate."

Years ago, my dad told me, "Son, if you ever feel like hitting your wife, it's time to leave." After she called me a cheapskate, I didn't say another word. I just walked. Five months later, we were officially divorced and my net worth had been reduced by ninety percent. Serves me right. That's what happens when you marry a girl you've dated for exactly three weeks.

We met back in '94. She was running cocktails at the Rio, where I used to go after work to waste a few quarters and unwind. She was the best-looking girl in the place, maybe in any place. Short blond hair, movie-star smile, and mysterious green cat's eyes that shimmered like emeralds when the light hit them a certain way. All packed into a smokin' little body made even more irresistible by the Rio's famous low-cut uniforms. To get her attention, I over-tipped like a crazy man, and she spent every break watching me play. I guess that's when she got the idea I was loaded.

In those days, we talked about everything, and she laughed at my jokes, and it seemed like we were the only two people in the world. Less than a month after we met, Joy and I slipped out for a few drinks one night when her shift was over. The next thing I knew, we were at the Burning Love Wedding Chapel, standing next to some rummy preacher while a second-rate Elvis impersonator sang "Love Me Tender" and tried to look down Joy's dress. Here in Vegas, that's what they mean by multi-tasking. Afterwards, we hopped on a charter flight to La Paz for the honeymoon, where all we did was screw and drink. What a pair to draw to, a lapsed Catholic and a jack Mormon.

When a professional poker player gets a hand that can't lose, he calls it "the nuts." That was us, at least in the early days. We were in love and life was better than I could have ever imagined. One night, we skipped the birth control and made ourselves a baby. I thought I'd hit the jackpot. Joy came to work at the bar and the customers flocked around just to get a look at her. Her tips were twice as good as at the Rio, even though she showed half as much flesh. She was raking it in and so was I. Even Bev was happy for us.

But something happened to Joy while she was pregnant. She got fat. Not just pregnant fat, but really fat. They tell me it happens. It bothered her more than it did me. I knew she'd get her shape back. But customers didn't look at her quite the same way anymore. She started brooding, complaining, accusing me of "doing this" to her. She began to worry about herself as a mother. And she started shopping. It all went south from there …

Bev's voice interrupted my bumpy trip down memory lane. "The man from the Health Department's here."

"At this hour?" I asked. "What's he want, a bigger bribe?" I spun on my heels to see, not the geek from the Health Department, but the newly crowned Sergeant Wally Zelasko, smiling like a fool.

"Gotcha good, didn't I?" he asked.

"Never piss off the proprietor," I said. "I'll have the waitress spit in your food."

"Which waitress?"

"The ugly one."

"Oh come on, Jimmy, you never hired an ugly waitress in your life."

"I will now, just to wait on you."

We shook hands and Wally clapped me on the back, nearly knocking the breath out of me. Except for the shiny bald noggin, he still looks like the same guy who played blocking fullback on our high school football team, the Paradise Pirates. At about five-nine, he's a head shorter than I am, but probably outweighs me by a good fifty pounds, most of it muscle.

I motioned to an empty table. "Why don't you sit here with all of your friends," I said. "I'll be right back."

As Wally slid into the booth, I stepped behind the bar to draw a pitcher of Michelob and to place his usual order, a Double Shamrock Burger, rare, and fries.

"Hey, Wally," I asked when I returned with our brew, "what sexual position produces the ugliest children?"

"I give up."

"Ask your mom."

He chuckled and, without missing a beat, asked, "What's the quickest way to clear a men's room?"

"What?"

"Say, 'Nice dick.' I heard that from the guys in vice."

"They should know. So, what brings you to our humble establishment? It's been too long."

"Yeah, I don't get out much these days. I guess you heard about the promotion."

"I suppose congratulations are in order."

"Thanks," he said with no enthusiasm. "You know, I figured it up the other day. I'm working longer hours. I've got a shitload more responsibility. And by the time they take out taxes and all that other junk, I'm barely making minimum wage."

"I could use another delivery driver," I offered.

"I'll keep that in mind. It's weird, now that I'm off the street, Evelyn's happy, the kids are happy, everybody's happy but me."

"They've got a word for that," I said. "It's called 'marriage'."

Wally said, "Amen," and drained half his glass in one gulp, wiping the foam from his mouth with the back of his catcher's-mitt hand. Just then, Brandi arrived with his order.

"Thanks, babe," Wally said.

"Can I get you anything else?" she asked.

"We'll let you know," I said.

"Okay, Mr. D."

"Jimmy."

"Okay, Jimmy." She gave us a shy half-smile as she retreated to the kitchen.

"Cute kid," Wally said.

"She's new."

"You laying the wood to that?"

"I'd like to, but you know me. I never get involved with the help."

"Yeah, right."

Ignoring him, I added, "But I might make an exception with her. I've been out of action way too long."

"That's not healthy." Wally took a monstrous bite out of his burger and I watched the juice trickle down the side of the bun and fall to his plate in little bloody droplets. "Just the way I like it," he said. "You remembered."

"I remembered, all right. Haven't you heard of E. coli?"

"It adds flavor," he said. The burger disappeared in two more mouthfuls. While he chewed, I plucked a French fry from his basket and popped it in my mouth.

"Help yourself," Wally said.

"Would you like to know why my fries are so good?" I asked.

Wally refilled his glass and answered, "It's the grease."

"How'd you know that?"

"Your dad taught you to change out the deep-friolator every other day, so the food won't absorb the old broken-down grease. He always said that even a fried shoe tastes delicious in fresh grease." He looked pleased with himself. "And you thought I wasn't listening."

Sometimes I forget that Wally's been hanging around almost as long as I have. When we were on the team, most of the players wouldn't have anything to do with me, because I was the kicker and the new kid, to boot. They never considered me to be a real athlete, even that time I nailed the game-winning field goal with three seconds on the clock. But my Pop, God bless him, started inviting them over for free pizza and Coke after the games, win or lose, and before long, I almost felt like one of the guys. After graduation, the rest of the players sort of drifted away, but Wally's been coming back ever since.

When he finished the last of his fries, he leaned back with a satisfied expression and said, "We need to talk about the break-in. Ramos told me you wouldn't let us speak to the help."

"Come on, Wally, look around you. Most of these people have been with me for years. Except for Brandi, and her parents are filthy rich. She's just slumming. Oh, and Jason, the new bus boy. But he's too stupid to think of something like that."

"Maybe he's got friends. Maybe Brandi's a klepto."

"I doubt it."

"Well then, old buddy, our hands are tied. You might want to consider hiring a security guard."

"Can't afford it."

"What about going partners with the other merchants?"

"Highly unlikely. But I'll ask around."

"You do that. I'd hate to see this place go under after all these years. You're my meal ticket."

"Wally, I never knew you were such a sentimental guy."

"It's my only fault." He snuck a quick peek at his watch and said, "Well, compadre, I'd better get home to the old ball and chain. Whenever I'm late, she's on the phone all night."

"Calling the station? The hospital?"

"No, my life insurance agent." He reached into his wallet and peeled off a ten for Brandi. What the hell—he didn't have to pay for the meal.

"Give my love to the family," I said, extending my hand.

"Handshakes are for fags," he said, crushing me in a big bear hug.

"Can't breathe," I gasped, doing my best 1950's B-movie impression. Must … have … air."

"I got your air right here."

In mock horror I said, "Beat it, Wally, before I call a cop."

"I hate cops."

"Me too."

On the way out, he dipped his hand into the cooler and emerged with a couple of Heinekens. "Put these on my tab," he said. Before I could think of something clever to say, he was gone.

5

Vegas gets about three comfortable days a year and Friday was one of them. No searing temperatures or sand storms or flash floods, just an unseasonably perfect seventy degrees accompanied by a gentle easterly breeze that blew the smog into California, where it belongs. If the hotel hotshots could find a way to package this weather and charge for it, they'd add a few more zeroes to their bottom line. Driving to the airport to pick up my daughter, I noticed the megaresorts had a fresh-scrubbed airbrushed quality that made them look especially enticing, the same way a Venus flytrap must look to its prey.

McCarran International Airport is, hands down, the most glamorous public facility I've ever seen. From the colossal corkscrew parking structure and the gleaming corridors to the high-tech trams whooshing passengers to the outlying gates, it's a cross between Disneyland and the Kennedy Space Center. Oh, and don't forget the slot machines, row upon row of bandits offering visitors the chance to lose their bankrolls before even stepping foot in a casino. As a local, I know those slots have the worst payouts this side of my late Uncle Patrick, who ran an illegal crap game back in Motown and who now rests in peace, rumor has it, as part of the Edsel Ford Expressway.

I got to the airport an hour early. I'm always nervous when Jenny flies, even though she's an old pro at this. The plane from

Salt Lake's a quickie 55-minute run, so it's not like she can get lost along the way, but I'm still a little old lady where my daughter's concerned. After checking the board to make sure her flight was on time, I planted myself at a nearby Starbucks, where I overpaid for a Vente decaf that tasted vaguely of cardboard. From my vantage point, I settled in for some serious people watching. At the gate to my immediate left, a boisterous party crowd deplaned with eager childlike anticipation, whooping and hollering as they raced through the concourse. At the gate to my right, their more subdued counterparts lay draped over the seats like wrinkled laundry, fighting hangovers or worse while waiting for their flights to Akron or Buffalo or wherever the hell they were going back to. I think we'd all be better off if they just handed their money over to me.

At 7 o'clock, I made my way toward the gate, anxious to stake out a premium spot. A half hour later, the plane still hadn't arrived and my stomach was doing flip-flops. For the third or fourth time, I asked the girl behind the counter if everything was okay, and with barely concealed annoyance, she assured me it was. Under different circumstances, I might have come on to her. She was a slender grad-school type who spoke softly, but was probably a screamer in bed.

"We're running a little behind is all" she said. "Just a minor mechanical problem in Salt Lake."

"What kind of mechanical problem?" I hoped that wasn't airline-speak for "the wings fell off and the jet is hurtling toward the ground like a meteor."

"Something to do with the ventilation system. Nothing to worry about," she said, forcing a smile that looked more like a grimace to me.

"You don't have kids, do you?"

"No, why?"

"Just a hunch."

The jet finally arrived at 8:05 and I gave a silent thanks to the patron saint of fucked-up flights. The first person off the plane was an ancient woman on crutches, followed by a teenage girl holding a screaming baby. And then Jenny, looking like Christmas, all green eyes like her Mom and red hair like her Dad, with a sunnier disposition than either of us, galloping out in front of a flight attendant who could hardly keep up. As soon as Jenny noticed me, a smile exploded across her face and I could see she'd lost another tooth since the last time we were together. Breaking free of the attendant's hand, she flew into my arms, shouting "Jimmy Daddy! Jimmy Daddy!" over and over. Lifting her over my head, I smothered her with kisses and said, "Hey, kiddo, you're getting big. I can hardly pick you up anymore."

"Oh, you're just old," she said, laughing. It's my favorite sound.

At last, the flight attendant caught up to us. At close range, I could see she was a pinched crone-like woman, and I briefly wondered if she'd worked with Lindbergh. It made me long for the days of age discrimination, when all the female airline personnel were hotties.

"And you are?" she asked.

"I'm the Dad."

"That's Jimmy Daddy," Jenny said, trying to be helpful.

The woman frowned slightly. I could tell it was her natural expression. "I'll need to see some identification, please," as if Jenny's exuberance wasn't proof enough.

"Sure," I said, producing my driver's license.

She stared at it for a long time, looked at me, then back at the photo.

"This license is expired," she said finally.

"Does that mean I can't have my daughter?"

She looked at me disapprovingly and said, "No, but I suggest you get it taken care of."

"Right away," I promised, snapping off what I thought was a crisp salute.

As soon as the woman left, Jenny said, "That lady's mean."

"Forget about her," I said. "How was your trip?"

"Bumpy. It was fun." She took my hand and we bounced our way downstairs to the baggage carousel, where her big green suitcase was already waiting for us.

Hefting it over the side, I grunted, "This thing weighs a ton. How long did you say you were staying?"

"I dunno. Two days, maybe."

"You truly are your mother's daughter."

"Yours too," she said.

"I'll have to teach you about traveling light."

"Be careful," she said. "There's a present in there for you."

"Really? What kind of present?"

"It's a surprise. I made it myself."

"Then I'm sure I'll love it."

In the car, I buckled Jenny in and asked, "Hungry?"

"Yeah. All they had to eat on the plane were peanuts. I hate peanuts."

"Where do you want to go?"

Her face lit up. "Jimmy D's!"

I tousled her hair and said, "Your Mom made me promise you wouldn't be hanging around there all weekend."

"Do we have to tell?"

"No. But we'll need a cover story."

"What's that?"

"It's, uh, sort of like a lie, but not as bad. Just a little fib so she won't get mad at us."

"Okay."

"Let's tell her we went to a Disney movie."

"Those are dumb."

"I know."

"What if she asks me about it?"

"They're all the same. Just say it's about some cute little monkey that gets lost and has to find its way back home."

Jenny smiled. "You're funny," she said. "Let's go to Jimmy D's, Jimmy Daddy! I want to play that darts game you taught me."

"All right," I said. "But don't beat me as bad as last time. I can't afford it."

We took the surface streets back to the bar. At this hour on a Friday night, I knew I-15 would be a parking lot, jammed with cash-laden tourists anxious to prop up the local economy.

Along the way, I casually asked Jenny, "So, your mother tells me she has a new, uh, guy friend." Normally, I have a rule against involving her in our adult dealings. She would grow up soon enough. But this time, curiosity was getting the better of me, and I couldn't resist. That twinge of regret was pinging me again, with Jenny bringing up all kinds of old memories. At least in the kid department, Joy and I had done all right for ourselves.

"You mean Uncle Roger?"

"Yeah, I guess. Is that what you call him?"

"Uh-huh. Mommy says it's better than poo-poo head."

I almost got a hernia stifling a laugh. "He can't be that bad, can he?"

Jenny frowned as she considered the question. "No, he's just boring. He tries to act all friendly and stuff, but I can tell he doesn't like kids."

"Maybe he's afraid of them."

"What does he think, I'll bite him?"

"Not with those teeth," I said. Jenny giggled and I decided to drop the interrogation before I made her uncomfortable.

We drove along for a few more miles. Finally, Jenny broke the silence. "Knock knock," she said.

"Who's there?"

"Cargo."

"Cargo who?"

"Cargo honk honk."

"Cute," I said, honking the horn for emphasis.

"Knock knock."

"Who's there?"

"Dishes."

"Dishes who?"

"Dishes me. Who ish you?"

"Ha ha."

"Knock knock."

"Aren't you done yet?"

"Knock knock."

"Who's there?"

"Cows."

"Cows who?"

"No, cows moo."

"Gee, now you're getting sophisticated."

"What's that mean?"

"You know, grown up. Adult."

Jenny looked proud of herself. "Knock knock."

"Last one, right?"

"Knock knock."

"I give up. Who's there?"

"Thistle."

"Thistle who?"

"Thistle be my last joke."

"Thank God. Here's one for you. Knock knock."

"Who's there?"

"Nobody."

"Nobody who?"

"Nobody."

She wrinkled her nose. "That's not even funny."

"I made it up myself."

"I can tell. Are we there yet?"

"Just a few more minutes. But if I don't get some gas, we'll spend the whole weekend right here." I turned left into the first station I saw, a Horrible Howie's. No wonder people back east think we're nuts. We've definitely got some weird-ass names. Like "Las Vegas," for instance. In Spanish, they tell me, it means "the meadows." In all the time I've lived here, I've never seen meadow one. Makes you wonder what the Spanish phrase is for "the parking lots."

The gas station was equipped with the latest pay-at-the-pump technology. I swiped my titanium Visa card (better than platinum! What's next, plutonium?) and waited for the quick approval. Instead, the digital message came back, "Declined." Annoyed, I swiped it again. Same response. What's the point of all this new stuff if it never friggin' works? Fine, I'll fix you, I thought. I whipped out the trusty no-limit American Express card and repeated the process. Again, "Declined."

Jenny stuck her head out the window and asked, "What's taking so long?"

"These pumps are all messed up. Stay in the car while I go inside and deal with it."

"Can I have a Coke?"

"How many have you had today?"

"Just one."

"When we get to Jimmy D's."

"Oh, all right."

Inside the convenience store, the dull-looking teenage boy behind the counter ignored me for a few minutes until I cleared my throat and said, "I'm from Horrible's corporate. May I have your last name please?"

Instinctively, his hand shot up to finger his name badge. "Why?"

"Just policy. We're doing spot inspections this week."

Slowly, the hand came down and he said, "Connors. Am I in trouble?"

"Not yet," I said. "What's wrong with the pumps?"

"Nothing," he stammered. "At least I don't think anything's wrong."

"Pump number three isn't accepting my state-of-the-art super-secret corporate credit card." I showed him the Amex card.

"How come it doesn't say 'Horrible's'?" he asked.

I put my finger to my lips. "Shhh, not so loud. I told you, it's a secret. I'm working undercover tonight."

"Oh. Well, nobody's complained about the pumps. Let me try." He took the card, ran it through his machine and stared at the display for a moment before returning the piece of plastic to me. "Declined," he said. "Sorry."

This was too weird. Recovering quickly, I said, "No problem. I was testing you."

"How'd I do?"

"Passed. With flying colors." I reached in my pocket and pulled out a twenty. "Let's go with cash, okay?"

He pressed a few buttons and said, "All set."

"Thanks, Connors. Keep up the good work."

Back at the car, I filled the tank, making a mental note not to go back inside this particular Horrible's ever again.

We got to Jimmy D's a little after nine. The place was standing-room only.

"Look who's here!" I announced to everyone within earshot, pointing to Jenny. "The boss." With that, the staff and patrons made their usual fuss, hugging her and giving her high fives and asking a hundred questions at once. "Since my daughter's going to be with us all weekend," I continued, "I want to remind all you assholes to watch your language."

"Sure thing, Jimmy," said Herb, the fat plumber who always occupies the third stool on the left. Herb must have been trolling for chicks, because he wore vertical stripes in an effort to look slimmer. The stripes were seriously outnumbered.

In the back of my mind, something about the bar didn't seem quite right. Then it hit me. No band.

"Where's the 'En Fuegos'?" I whispered to Bev.

"I tried reaching you on your cell phone …"

"It's busted."

"Anyway, Lenny called. He said they're not coming in tonight because you bounced a check."

"Impossible!"

"Well, that's what he said. I suggested they show up regardless and we'd pay cash, but he said they already had other plans."

"Fuck 'em. They're fired. I never thought they were that good to begin with." The strange feeling I got at the gas station crept over me again. Then the thought I'd had on the night of the break-in intruded into my consciousness, and again I had to push it aside. I said to Bev, "Call Owen first thing Monday morning and have him find out what the hell's wrong with the bank." Owen's my ex-brother-in-law, married to Joy's sister Sarah. Even though we're no longer related, and he's not the greatest accountant, I keep him on because he's been with me for years. And he works cheap.

"No problem," Bev said.

I reached into the cash register and came up with a handful of quarters for Jenny, who was teasing Herb the plumber. "Why don't you go stick these in the juke box? I got a whole bunch of new Beach Boys songs just for you."

"Cool," she said.

On her last visit, I introduced Jenny to the classics by giving her my "Endless Summer" CD. She put on a little show for me, lip synching to "California Girls" and making up a cute little dance routine. Rumor has it she's driving her mother crazy.

After a few moments, I could hear the sounds of "Fun Fun Fun" over the noise of the crowd. When Jenny returned, I plopped her down in my personal seat at the far end of the bar. Bev lobbed me one of her patented disapproving looks, but I brushed it off. I know Jenny's not supposed to sit at the bar, but I'll take my chances. After all, these are childhood memories we're creating here.

"What are you having?" I asked her.

"A hamburger and fries. Make it like Uncle Wally's."

"That's disgusting," I said. "You're getting it medium-well like a normal person."

"Don't forget my Coke."

"Yes, ma'am."

Next to Jenny, two of my regulars were engaged in a game of mortal bar-bet combat. Dave and Stan are a couple of the smartest guys I've ever met. They know everything—except how to get a date or keep a job.

"Okay, smartass," Stan said. "Who's got zip code one two three four five?"

"Piece of cake," said Dave. "Schenectady."

"Son of a bitch."

"I got one for you, you bastard."

"Keep it clean," I warned.

"Sorry," Dave said, glancing at Jenny.

"It's okay," Jenny said. "Mommy says that all the time. When she's driving."

Dave continued, "Since we're on the subject of mothers, what famous product did Michael Nesmith's mom invent?"

"Michael Nesmith the Monkee?"

"No, Michael Nesmith the King of France. Of course, the Monkee. Quit your stalling."

"Can I get a hint?"

"What do I look like, information?"

"Just a little hint."

"You probably use this product every day."

"That rules out deodorant and mouthwash," I chimed in.

Stan looked hurt. "You don't have to insult me."

"I couldn't resist."

"I've got it!" Stan yelled. "Post-It Notes."

"Nope," Dave said. "Liquid Paper. You owe me another beer."

"Really? Liquid Paper? She must have made a bundle."

"No doubt."

"You'd think she could've afforded music lessons for her son."

"You're such a doofus," Dave said. "Nesmith was the only Monkee who could play. All right, double or nothing. What was the name of his group after the Monkees?"

"What are you, queer for the guy?"

"Look who's talking, Mr. I-Haven't-Felt-Up-A-Girl-Since-High-School."

I could see where this was heading, so I made a beeline for the kitchen to retrieve Jen's order. On the way, I motioned to Mick the bartender, saying, "Keep an eye on those two. It could get ugly." Mick's not much taller than a jockey, but he's the toughest guy I know. He was an MP in the Army before an ironic reversal of fortune landed him in the stockade for three months.

Mick gave me a wink and said, "I got the Equalizer right here." The Equalizer is a black 32-ounce aluminum Louisville Slugger with a nasty-looking dent in the barrel from one brief incident years ago. At the time, my old man added to its mystique by smearing a dollop of red paint right on the business end, along with a little clump of Barbie hair. I guess it sends the proper message, because we've never had to use the damn thing since.

Jenny and I had a terrific night. We always do. After dinner, we played electronic darts, where she beat me three out of three. I don't have to pretend to lose, because I stink. Months ago, when I first taught Jenny how to play, Joy gave me the usual hard time.

"That's not an appropriate game for a little girl."

"It's better than pool."

"The only reason you haven't stuck a cue in her hand is because she's too short."

"I can't see where it's hurting her any. Besides, it's good for her math skills." Not bad, I thought. How do I come up with these things?

Joy wasn't having any of it. But sure enough, on Jenny's next report card, her math grade shot up from a C to a B+. Score one for Dad.

When we finished our game, I switched one of the TVs to ESPN2, where they were showing some sort of women's gymnastics. Jenny loves gymnastics. After a few of the regulars groaned, I said, "Stick a cork in it. You've got eleven other screens to choose from."

"Hey, Jimmy," Herb said. "I know how they can get higher ratings."

"Does it involve taking their clothes off?" I asked.

"Naturally."

"Don't listen to him," I said to Jenny. "He's a very bad man." Jenny just laughed.

"Just think of it," Herb said. "It would give a whole new meaning to the term 'triple lutz.'"

"That's a figure-skating term, you moron," said Dave, who had obviously grown tired of insulting Stan. "Don't you know anything?"

"Butt out," Herb warned. "I'm serious, Jimmy. They could put it on pay-per-view. I'd buy it."

"Herb," I said, "you have an illegal cable box. You've never bought anything in your life."

"It's the principle of the thing," he said, going back to his beer, which he did, admittedly, pay for.

Just after ten o'clock, Jenny informed me, "I'm bored of this. Can I play office?"

"It's awfully late," I said.

"Please?" she asked. "That's the magic word, right?"

I caved in immediately. "Well, okay. I can never resist the magic word."

Depositing Jenny behind my desk, I fixed her up with stacks of obsolete credit-card slips, outdated inventory forms and junk mail, plus scissors, Scotch tape, stapler, letter opener, and pens in an assortment of ink colors. Surrounded by all that stuff, she looked just like any other seven-year-old CEO.

"Thanks, Jimmy Daddy!" she squealed.

While she bossed around her crew of imaginary employees, I got out the checkbook.

Jenny glanced up from her papers and asked, "Whatcha doing?"

"Oh, just writing a check out to myself. We'll need some cash for the weekend, in case we decide to do something fun."

With a serious expression, she said, "Why don't you get money from the safe like Uncle Owen?"

"That money goes into the bank," I explained. "He puts it in this bag when he goes to make a deposit." I pointed to a gray vinyl bank bag on top of the filing cabinet.

Jenny shook her head. "No, I mean, like when he puts it in his pocket," she said.

I just stared at her. "He does?"

"Yeah, I saw him do it last time I was here," she said, promptly losing interest and returning to her deskwork. "Do you have an eraser?"

"Top drawer," I said absentmindedly. I was sure Jenny was mistaken about Owen. Still, I'd find a way to ease it into the conversation the next time I saw him.

I checked up on Jenny every twenty minutes or so. Sometime around midnight, she crapped out. Gently, I lifted her sleeping form out of my chair and carried her to the small air mattress I keep wedged in one corner of the office. Back when Joy used to lock me out of the house, that mattress and I logged quite a few hours together.

"I won't be long, kiddo," I whispered as I tucked her in. She made a soft whimpering noise and I thought I could see the trace of a smile. "Sweet dreams," I said, kissing her on the forehead.

I went back out to the bar with an extra bounce in my step. "It doesn't get any better than this," I said to myself. And, for once, I was right.

6

Monday mornings are never easy. This one was worse than most. I sat like a lump at my desk, staring forlornly at the Popsicle-stick pencil holder Jenny had made for me in art class, and replayed our parting airport conversation. Just before I put her on the flight back to Salt Lake, I could see it coming. But like a fastball aimed right at my head, I couldn't get out of the way.

"Jimmy Daddy," she said with a slight crack in her voice.

"What, sweetheart?"

"Why can't I stay here with you?"

I sighed. "We've been over this before. The judge says you have to live with Mommy."

Now the dam broke and her tears flowed freely. "I hate the judge!" she said.

"Me, too. She's a witch with a 'b'. But we have to do what she says. Besides, you've got your home and your friends and school and ..."

"But I want to be with you. I could help at Jimmy D's."

Now it was my turn to choke back a tear. "That's the nicest thing anybody ever said to me," I told her. "But you're too young. I'd get in trouble. You wouldn't want that, would you?"

She shook her head slowly. "I guess not."

"When you're older, we'll work together. And then, someday, if you want, I'll give the bar to you."

Jenny stopped crying. "Honest?"

"I promise." I took out a Kleenex and wiped her nose. "That's better. We can't have you representing the Delaney family on this flight with snot running all over the place."

She giggled and said, "I love you, Jimmy Daddy."

"I love you too, honey. Call me when you get home."

"Seven oh two, three four four, two six eight four. I memorized it."

"Good," I said. "It's the most important number you'll ever learn."

We hugged for somewhere between an instant and an eternity, and I reluctantly handed her over to the Southwest flight attendant, who was trying hard not to eavesdrop.

"Take good care of my daughter," I instructed.

"It's my specialty," she said, and I felt her concern.

I gave a little half-hearted wave and bounded for the tram, trying to remember where I parked the damned car.

Now, though, I had to put all that behind me as Bev filled me in on the morning's activities.

"The Bud guy's five cases short, but he said he'll have them for us tomorrow. And Marty from Triumph Wholesale dropped off the wrong ground beef. It looks like something from my old high-school cafeteria."

"Get him on the horn and tell him that's unacceptable. We're not the fucking Burger Barn, for chrisake."

"Already taken care of."

"Typical Monday, huh Bev?"

"You said it."

"Any luck finding a new band?"

"I set up an audition with a group called the Rolling Blackouts. They're a classic rock band out of L.A."

"Good. That reminds me, did you talk to Owen about that bounced check?"

"I left a message."

"Let me know as soon as he calls."

"Well, even if he doesn't, he's supposed to be in at three to go over the books."

"Like we're not busy enough. Bev, you're a jewel. I don't know what I'd do without you."

"You'd go right down the shitter, that's what you'd do."

"I love it when you talk dirty." Like a shooting star, a flash of red streaked across her face and then flew out of her mouth.

"Jimmy Delaney, Jr., someday that wise-ass attitude of yours is going to get you in trouble!"

"Don't count on it," I said. "I'm too fast on my feet."

Bev slammed the door on her way out, rattling the business license and other assorted debris hanging on the wall.

It was still an hour before the lunch rush. Just enough time to knock on a few doors and try to drum up support for a security guard.

First stop, Santini's Italian Bakery. Mrs. Santini, a stout woman with beauty-shop blue hair, looked up from her dough when she heard the tinkling of the bell.

"Oh, it's you," she said.

"Nice to see you, too, Mrs. Santini," I said in my most pleasant voice.

"I was hoping you were a customer. It's been pretty slow around here."

"Don't I always buy something, Mrs. S?"

"Yes."

"Then that makes me a customer, doesn't it?"

Frowning, she said, "There you go again with the logic. Always trying to confuse me."

"How's the canolis today?" I asked.

"Same as ever. Fresh and delicious."

"I'll take a half-dozen."

While she filled my bag, I said, "You heard I got broken into again the other night."

"Of course," she said with a sour expression. "They busted down my back door to get to you. My deductible's too high, so it's not covered." She made it sound like it was my fault.

Still, I sensed my opening. "That's what I wanted to talk to you about. The police think we should hire a security guard."

She shook her head. "The police are idiots. They don't do their job."

"I agree. That's why I was thinking—"

"How much does a guard cost?"

That was a good sign. When they start asking about money, it means they're interested.

"I don't know. Eight, ten bucks an hour. If all the merchants go in, we're only looking at about seventy dollars a week each."

"I have to sell a lot of bread to make seventy dollars."

"I can appreciate that, Mrs. S, but—"

"Well, since you're the only one who seems to be having this problem, I think you should pay." She dismissed me with a wave of her flour-covered hand. "I think you should reimburse me for my door, too."

So much for the diplomatic approach. Getting steamed, I said, "You're lucky I buy your crappy canolis!" I slammed a ten-dollar bill on the counter and stormed out.

My luck was no better at Getaway Travel, where Tom Grogan, the little shit of a manager, had other concerns. Grogan's one of those guys who's got everything figured out. Meanwhile, he's making thirty thou a year max and wearing polyester suits from JC Penney.

Sporting his usual know-it-all smirk, he said, "Those guards aren't too bright, you know."

"I didn't know."

"They're just a bunch of big stupid lunks who couldn't make the force. Shoot first, ask questions later. It's blood lust, plain and simple. Before you know it, you've got a lawsuit on your hands."

"Maybe we could get a nice older fellow who's a retired cop or something."

"Probably blind as a bat. Next thing I know, I've got a bullet in my chest."

"Not such a bad idea," I muttered.

"How's that?"

"Nothing. Thanks for your time, Tom."

"I have to tell you, Jimmy, you're looking a little tense. I've got some dynamite vacation packages. How about a nice cruise to the Mexican Riviera? Go down to Cabo, get in a little fishing, try your luck with the local señoritas, if you know what I mean."

"Is that all in the brochure?"

"Pretty much. Except for the señoritas."

"I'll look it over." He handed me some literature, which I threw in the trash can right outside his front door, and I hope he saw me. But there I was, oh-for-two and it wasn't even noon yet. I decided to skip the Chinese laundry, where they pretended not to speak English, and go back to work. My powers of persuasion might be at an all-time low, but at least I could still cook.

Lunch hour came and went. Then, at three on the nose, my ex-brother-in-law Owen shuffled in. He's dependable as an atomic clock, a tall long-limbed man of forty, with stooped shoulders, a serious demeanor, and four daughters. If I had four girls, I'd probably be serious, too. When I think of Jenny, I can't imagine trying to divide that love four ways. Who knows, maybe it multiplies. I'm not sure that's the case with Owen, but it's hard to tell when you're on the outside looking in.

"I'm not worth a darn," he once told me. "Can't make a son to save my life." He and Sarah, Joy's older sister, are devout Mormons. In fact, Owen's some kind of bishop at his church, which he says places a premium on boys. "I'd try again, but Sarah's not up for it. And to be honest with you, I can barely afford the ones we've got. Girls are expensive. It's Calvin Klein this and Gap that. You can't just buy them Levis and a T-shirt and send them off to school."

"Luckily, Jenny's not at that stage yet."

"Give her time."

"I thought you people crafted your own crude clothing out of scraps of material," I said. "Or sheep."

Owen just chuckled. "Where'd you hear that?"

"Donny and Marie, I think."

"Well, that's just a rumor started by the Catholics."

Today, Owen was even more serious than usual. He looked like a guy who wasn't getting a whole lot of sleep. When we shook hands, his palms felt cold and clammy.

"Everything okay?" I asked.

"Yeah, fine," he said, staring into the distance.

Owen's seven-year-old has been a sick little girl for as long as I can remember. Some sort of ten-syllable blood thing that's constantly going in and out of remission. I'm uncomfortable bringing the subject up, but always feel like I should ask.

"How's Rachel?"

He looked at me with mild surprise. "She's doing great," he said, smiling for the first time. "No trace of anything at her last check-up."

"That's good news," I said.

Owen studied me for a moment. "You're the only one who asks anymore," he said. "Most people never even mention it."

"Maybe they're afraid to."

"Or they don't remember," he shrugged.

"In my book, there's nothing worse than having a sick kid. I don't know how you guys do it."

"You just do, that's all. There's no other choice. Keep the faith, like the hippies used to say." He paused, then added, "Speaking of faith, why don't you join us tomorrow for a bible study group. We're discussing—"

I couldn't cut him off fast enough. "Oh, no, you don't," I said. "That's the last place I want to be."

"I just thought it might do you some good."

"Listen," I told him, "the Mormons don't need somebody like me. I could single-handedly bring down the whole religion."

"You over-estimate yourself, Jimmy. We've seen worse."

"Fine. I'll bring the beer."

Owen rubbed his tired eyes. "You're hopeless."

"That's what I've been trying to tell you." Changing the subject, I said, "I suppose you heard about the burglary."

"Of course."

"You wanna know the worst part? I don't have enough insurance. I've been thinking, maybe I should let you handle all my stuff, not just the books."

Owen's eyebrows darted up and down. "Funny you should mention that," he said. "I've been considering branching out. In fact, I just finished an extension course at UNLV about how to position myself as a business consultant. They say that's where the money is. Lord knows I could use it, what with the medical bills and all."

"Let's talk about that next week," I said. "I'd love not having to deal with all the bullshit anymore. In the meantime, the desk's all yours. If you need to clean it off, just throw in a match."

"Right." He pulled a pair of reading glasses from his pocket, adjusting them on the bridge of his nose. All he needed was one of those green eyeshades to complete the picture.

"By the way, did you call the bank about that bounced check to the band?"

"It's handled," he assured me. "They made a mistake in their data entry. I even got them to credit back the NSF fee."

"You the man."

Smiling weakly, he said, "Tell that to my wife."

Only later did I realize I'd forgotten to ask him about that business with the safe. No big deal. There'd be plenty of time for that.

7

"Owen's missing," Sarah managed to croak between sobs. She sat in my office, dabbing at her eyes with a wadded-up tissue that had reached its saturation point.

As I handed her a fresh one, I couldn't help noticing what a good-looking woman she still was, even with red puffy eyes and four daughters. Sarah's the "Nice Sister." She and Joy couldn't be less alike if they were two randomly selected strangers. Except in the looks department, where they're practically twins. It gave me the creeps. That blonde green-eyed stuff didn't do it for me anymore.

"What do you mean 'missing'?" I asked.

"He didn't come home last night."

"That's not like him."

"I'm so worried. He was here yesterday afternoon, wasn't he?"

"Yes."

"What time did he leave?"

"Five, five-thirty tops. I hate to ask, but did you check all the hospitals?"

"Of course. Nobody came in matching his description."

"What about the cops?"

"No help," she said angrily. At least that was better than crying. "They told me there's usually a logical explanation. Excessive drinking, a girlfriend, that sort of thing. But Owen would never do anything like that."

I nodded in agreement.

Sarah continued, "The police couldn't have been less helpful. They won't even let me fill out a missing persons report for the first twenty-four hours. It's just so frustrating, I can't stand it! If anything's happened to Owen, I don't know how I'll go on. And the girls …" The sentence trailed off into another round of tears.

When she regained her composure, I asked, "Have you talked to Joy yet?"

"No. I don't want to worry her unnecessarily."

"Probably a good idea," I said, imagining how my ex-wife would overreact. "Can I get you a glass of wine?"

"You know I don't drink." Forcing a smile, she added, "But this might be a good time to start."

"One snifter of Jimmy D's private-reserve medicinal sherry coming right up."

When I returned with the wine, Sarah reached for it with a trembling hand and downed it in one gulp.

"Yuck," she said, making a face.

"Just what the doctor ordered."

"Don't tell Owen I did this," she said. The alcohol was already turning the tips of her ears a bright red.

"I promise. Sarah, has Owen seemed different lately?"

She considered the question before answering, "Not different, really. Maybe quieter, a little more distant."

"Listen," I said. "I have a friend at Metro. A sergeant. He owes me about five hundred favors. Why don't I give him a call and have him nose around? In the meantime, you go home and try to get some rest. I'm sure everything will be fine. You know, they'll probably find Owen at the Bunny Ranch with a bunch of hookers."

Sarah's mouth fell open and she stared at me, uncomprehending.

"Dumb joke," I said. "Never mind."

"That's okay, Jimmy. You're a good ex-brother-in-law. I wish you and Joy were still together."

"You're the only one who does," I said. "But thanks for the sentiment."

I got on the speakerphone and buzzed Bev. "Who's delivering today?"

"Jeremy."

"What's he driving?"

Bev yelled something and I could hear a muffled voice respond, "Mustang."

"Good," I said. "Have him drive Sarah home. And throw in a large pizza."

"I couldn't," Sarah said, holding her hands out in protest.

"Nonsense. You can't possibly drive after all that booze. I bet you're over the legal limit already." I had to chuckle to myself over her one little shot of sherry.

"But what about my car?"

"I'll have it dropped off later."

"Thanks, Jimmy." She got up and quickly kissed my cheek. "I feel a little better already."

"That's what I'm here for," I said. "I'll call you the minute I hear something."

As soon as Sarah left, I dialed Wally's direct number.

"Zelasko," he said gruffly.

"Wally, lose the official voice. It's Jimmy."

"Hey, bud, what's up?"

"Here's the deal. My ex-brother-in-law Owen never came home last night. He's a nice religious boy, so he's probably not out raising hell. His wife tried to report it, but all she got was the normal bullshit. See what you can dig up, will you?"

After I gave him Owen's description and other vital statistics, Wally said, "I'm on it. But this'll cost you."

"Doesn't it always?"

I hung up and sat there for a while, thinking. Despite my assurances to Sarah, the knot in my stomach told me that everything probably *wasn't* all right. A guy like Owen doesn't just disappear. Unless he's dead. In Vegas, anything can happen. A random shooting, case of mistaken identity, carjacking. He could be in a trunk or a dumpster or buried out in the desert behind a cactus. It almost happened to me years ago. Right before closing time, some guy followed me into the bathroom, stuck a gun in my face, and made off with my wallet. I guess he didn't realize I owned the place or he would have gotten a lot more. But the point is, maybe the bad guy doesn't like my looks, or I don't have enough money on me, or he's just nervous and strung out, and bang, in less than a second I'm dead on my own bathroom floor. It just goes to show, when you leave the house in the morning, there's no guarantee you're coming home.

8

The call from the bank ruined my Tuesday morning and it wasn't even ten o'clock yet. You'd think I'd be used to bad news by now, but I wasn't. In fact, I was giving serious thought to yanking the phone out of the wall and strangling myself with the cord.

"Mr. Delaney?" a timid voice asked.

"You got him."

"It's Iris Sanders. From Nevada National."

"Hi, Iris." I sort of remembered her. A little on the mousy side, but take off those big glasses and she's definitely doable. "How's my money?"

She hesitated for a moment before saying, "Well, that's the reason I'm calling. There's a problem with your account."

Just like during my last losing streak, I could feel the old familiar pressure building up in my head. It started at the base of my skull and spread, like fungus, to my temples, before settling in behind my eyes. "What kind of problem?"

"We're showing fourteen checks with non-sufficient funds and a negative balance of seven hundred ninety-three dollars and fifty-four cents."

"That can't be right. I always keep five grand in that account. Just in case."

"I can see that."

"Well, why don't you guys look into it?"

"That's what we're trying to do—"

"In the meantime, can't you just transfer the funds from savings to cover the checks? I thought you did that automatically."

"We do. But there's no money in your savings account, either."

"What?" I exploded. God, I needed a cigarette. But all I had was that worthless gum.

"I said, there's—"

I cut her off. "I heard you. Listen, I have no fucking idea what's going on here. Pardon my goddamn French, Iris, but there's supposed to be twenty-five thousand dollars in savings. This has to be a mistake. Are you sure you've got the right Delaney?"

"Yes, sir. James Delaney, Junior. Black Irish Enterprises, DBA Jimmy D's Saloon and Supper Club."

"Yeah, that's me," I had to admit. "How could this happen? Who in God's name took my money?"

Iris hesitated a moment before saying, "Well, there's no telling. But we do send monthly statements enumerating all of your credits and debits. Are you still at the West Sahara address?"

"Yeah, I haven't gone anywhere."

"Then you must have received our correspondence."

As Iris spoke, I began rifling through my desk drawers and filing cabinets, furiously searching for anything even remotely resembling a bank statement. The only thing I had to show for my efforts was a paper cut.

"Son of a bitch!"

"Mr. Delaney, are you all right?" Iris asked tentatively.

"I'll call you back," I said, shattering the phone against the desk. "Bev, get your ass in here!"

"You don't need to yell."

"Did you hear any of that conversation?" I stuck my bleeding thumb in my mouth.

"Was I supposed to?"

"That was the bank. They say I'm out of money."

Bev looked as shocked as I felt. "How can that be?"

"That's what I'd like to know. They said they've tried to notify me. Who gets that mail?"

"Owen."

"Great," I said. "Call the morgue and tell them I need to talk to him."

"Jimmy, that's not very nice," Bev scolded. "Even for you."

"I know. I'm more than a little pissed off right now."

"Can I offer a suggestion?"

"That's why you make the big bucks. Correction, *made* the big bucks."

"Call the bank again and ask them to fax over the records for the last three months or so," she said. "You know, all the deposits and withdrawals. Maybe that will tell us something."

"Good idea. Glad I thought of it."

I called, and a half hour later, the pages began to whir off the fax machine. The story they told was not a happy one.

Every two or three days for the past three months, a substantial amount of money had been withdrawn from my account: $500, $800, $1,400. Always nice round numbers, and always leaving a small balance. Until a few days ago, that is, when the remainder of the funds disappeared. No swamp or canal had ever been drained more methodically. Incredibly, all the signs pointed to Owen. He was the only one, other than myself, who had access. I added him to the account years ago so I wouldn't have to sign so many checks.

So. Maybe my ex-brother-in-law wasn't dead after all. Maybe he'd been contributing to his own personal retirement fund all along, planning a fast getaway when the timing was right. But why now? And what about Sarah and the girls, especially Rachel? Come to think of it, what about me?

Bev had been looking over my shoulder the whole time. Now, she let out a slow whistle and, as if reading my mind, said, "Well, it could be worse."

"How, exactly?" I demanded. The last thing I felt like hearing right now was a dose of unfounded optimism.

"You've got a bunch of equity in this place. I'm sure you can get a quick loan to bail us out. And who knows? The cops might find Owen with all the cash."

"Don't count on it," I said. "I think we underestimated Mr. Owen Johnson. And I don't like the loan idea. You remember what my Pop used to say about borrowing money against the business."

"Jimmy, I'm not sure we have a choice."

It was an effort just to shrug. "Okay, call Dean at the bank and set up an appointment. Tell him if he gives me this loan, I'll join the fucking Rotary."

It must have worked, because two hours later, I found myself sitting across a massive mahogany desk from Dean Cunningham, Vice-President of Nevada National, "Your Hometown Bank." I think I read in the paper that a Japanese firm had recently bought up the place, but they hadn't gotten around to changing the slogan yet. Dean, a fiftyish man almost as big as his desk, peered over his glasses at my "Fastrack" loan application, while I tried not to fidget. I've always hated sitting in these huge offices with the fancy artwork and important-looking documents on the walls. It makes me feel like I'm back in junior high, getting reamed by the Boy's Vice Principal.

After a few more minutes, Cunningham stuck a fleshy thumb under one suspender and said, "Looks good, Jimmy. All except these negative account balances."

"With all due respect, Dean, that's why I need the loan. I'm sure Bev told you, I've been embezzled. That's a financial term, isn't it?"

"Also a legal one. Have you called the police?"

"Yes. They're sending somebody over as soon as they're done writing speeding tickets."

"Well, I don't see any problem here. I'll call you in the morning and tell you when you can pick up your check."

I allowed myself to feel just a shred of relief. "Thanks, Dean. I really appreciate it."

We shook hands. As I turned to leave, he said, "Jimmy …"

"Yes?"

"Rotary's next Tuesday."

9

I never made it to Rotary. Dean called less than an hour later. "We have a problem."

"We do?" I asked. "What kind of problem?" The head pressure was starting again. I popped another piece of nicotine gum in my mouth and bit my tongue.

"Well, I'm sorry to have to tell you this, especially because we've known each other such a long time and you being a steady customer and all, but …"

"Dean, cut to the chase. I can handle it."

I heard him take a breath. "We can't give you the loan because the IRS has a lien on the bar."

I had been pacing back and forth in my office, but now I had to sit down.

Like an idiot, I repeated, "The IRS? The tax guys?" For a second, I thought he'd said the IRA, as in Irish Republican Army. I'm not sure who's worse.

"Yes, Jimmy. Apparently, they think you owe them back payroll taxes."

"But I pay my taxes. Like clockwork. It's a chunk of change, too. Owen fills out the paperwork and cuts the checks and … oh, fuck!"

"I beg your pardon?"

"That fucking Owen. He never mailed those checks. I am *so* screwed."

"It would appear," Cunningham said.

"Can I ask you something?"

"Anything."

"What should I do now?"

"If I were you, I'd go out and get myself a good tax attorney."

"Do you know any?"

"As a matter of fact, I do. Lloyd Chambers, Esquire. He's the best, works with all the major casinos. Ordinarily, he doesn't take on any new clients, but I have a feeling he'll help you."

"Why's that?"

"Let's just say we have some leverage where his mortgage is concerned."

Dean must have felt guilty about the loan, because he did a fine job of greasing the skids with Chambers, who could squeeze me in on Friday. In the meantime, Bev and I decided to maintain the illusion that everything was fine. It would be business as usual at Jimmy D's. No need to upset the troops until the feds hitched up a tractor-trailer to the bar and hauled it away to impound.

The only other person who knew the truth was Wally. I called to alert him that the search for Owen had taken an unexpected detour. Instead of a dead body, perhaps they should be looking for a live embezzler. He assured me that the guys from fraud would be paying me a visit soon, but so far, no sign of them. That told me where I stood in the grand scheme of things. And I'm supposed to be a man with connections.

I also thought it was better to stonewall Sarah for the time being. I felt she'd rather hope that her husband wasn't dead than know for certain he was a crook. She'd find out the truth soon enough and it was going to be damned hard on her. As it was, I could tell from her voice that she was barely keeping things together.

You could say the same about me. The strain was really starting to grind me down. I handled it by taking up an old hobby, drinking. After hours, I'd sit at the bar with a bottle of Midleton Very Rare Irish Whiskey. This bottle isn't for customers. It's only for special occasions, such as whenever my life falls apart.

As I worked on my third shot, lost in a seemingly endless spiral of "what ifs," a voice from behind startled me so badly I nearly fell off my seat.

"Evening, Jimmy."

I whirled around to find Pete, a homeless guy who stops in occasionally for leftovers. According to the Clark County Health Department, I'm to dispose of all uneaten cooked food in the appropriate manner, but I haven't got the heart. I met Pete a couple years ago when I opened the door to my storage shed, discovered him taking a siesta, and scared the living shit out of each other. From what he's told me, he once was a successful stockbroker until one day something snapped and they found him running down the halls in nothing but a yellow power tie, singing the Notre Dame fight song. Needless to say, his family stuck him in a psycho unit. Months later, he wandered off when nobody was looking and now he's just another old street person who looks like Jesus on a bad hair day. Pete doesn't always make sense, but when he does, he makes more sense than anyone.

"Pete, you've got to stop sneaking up on people. You practically gave me a heart attack."

"I know CPR," he said.

"You're a man of many talents. Pull up a stool and I'll pour you the finest Irish whiskey ever to cross your lips."

He sat and I measured out a double, which he drained with professional ease. Then, for just a few moments, he closed his eyes, smacked his lips, and rocked back and forth like Stevie Wonder on acid. The look on his face told the whole story; it was absolutely angelic.

"Not bad, huh?"

He opened his eyes wide and said in a tone approaching reverence, "It tastes like a liquid cloud."

"You, my friend, are a real poet. Are you sure you're not Irish?" I started to pour him another, but he waved me off.

"How can you improve on perfection?" he explained.

"Well, I'm giving it the old college try. Salud! That's an old Gaelic term." I emptied my glass.

"La chaim. That's Spanish. You can always tell when it starts with 'la'."

"I skipped that class, Pete." The fog was starting to roll in and blanket my brain. In another few minutes, I wouldn't be able to feel my lips.

Pete fixed me with a watery stare and said, "Jimmy, you don't look happy." That's what I like about the mentally ill; they're so direct.

"I got problems, Pete," I said, and instantly regretted it, adding, "but, hey, I should know better than to complain to a homeless man." Somehow, that didn't come out quite right, either. Luckily, Pete wasn't insulted.

"Believe it or not, Jimmy, I have fewer problems than anybody I know."

"Really?"

"Uh huh. No job, no bills, no taxes, no bullshit. Just this day that God made. Don't get me wrong, it's no walk in the park. Well, actually, it is a walk in the park. I walk there all the time. Sleep there, too. You know that park around the corner? The one next to the school? The sprinklers come on before sunrise. I think that's where they get the expression, 'rude awakening.' Now, what was my point?" He stopped for a second to regroup. "Oh yeah, if you ever want to live completely in the moment, try being homeless for a while."

"Thanks for the advice, Pete. You never know, I might be joining you. Maybe you could show me the ropes, be my mentor."

He considered it. "Mentor. I like the sound of that. Pass down the tricks of the trade to the younger generation." Suddenly turning serious, Pete asked, "Things that bad, Jimmy?"

"Well, I got broken into, my accountant embezzled all my money, and the IRS has a lien on the bar. That's bad, right?"

"But you don't have cancer," Pete said.

Squinting at him, I asked, "What's that got to do with anything?"

"I always figure, if you don't have cancer, it's a pretty good day."

"I guess you're right. No cancer, as far as I can tell."

"Good. Cause that stuff'll kill you."

I had to laugh, probably for the first time in days. Through the haze, the sound seemed to come from somewhere else.

"Pete, what do you want for dinner? I've got burgers and pizza tonight."

He produced a tattered paper shopping bag from inside his grimy windbreaker. "Just fill 'er up, Jimmy boy. And hold the gravy."

10

On Friday morning, I picked out my best blue blazer, least wrinkled khakis, and an old but expensive pair of Italian loafers. I wanted to look good for my 9:30 appointment at Drake, Elias, Chambers and McCloud, the noted Las Vegas tax attorneys. Luckily, I gave myself plenty of time, because a fender bender turned the ten-minute trip downtown into a half-hour ordeal. I'm always amazed how people will slow down to watch two idiots exchange insurance information. Cursing all the way, I pulled up to the converted ranch-style house on 7th Street at exactly 9:29. The homes in that neighborhood were built before World War II, which makes them historical monuments by Las Vegas standards. I figure they're scheduled for implosion any day now.

"James Delaney," I told the receptionist, "here for my appointment with Mr. Chambers." I tried to picture her naked, but couldn't get a good sense of her body under the conservative gray business suit. Should I take a chance? Maybe a quickie was just what I needed to change my luck. Or maybe not. I had a feeling it would be hard to get rid of her the next morning. With a passive expression, she punched a button and spoke into the intercom, "Your nine-thirty's here."

A disembodied voice answered, "I'm just finishing up a call. Tell him I'll be a few minutes."

"Please have a seat," the receptionist said. "It won't be long."

"Thanks," I said, giving her a wink. I folded myself into an overstuffed chair that could have been a refugee from an exclusive men's club. Passing on the assortment of financial magazines bound in impressive covers, I chose instead to take a closer look at my surroundings. It was, in the immortal words of my Pop, "some joint." Real hardwood floors, expensive art signed and numbered by foreign guys, a leather couch that probably took the lives of an entire herd of Texas's finest. Which made me realize, somebody has to pay for all this shit. Soon enough, that somebody would be me. Thank God today's consultation was free.

While I pondered my shaky financial future, a door opened and out strode a tall slender man with round wire glasses and too much hair, combed straight back and moussed to a black-lacquer finish. He couldn't have been more than thirty.

"Mr. Delaney?" he asked, sticking out his hand.

"Call me Jimmy," I said. "Mr. Chambers?"

The man chuckled. "No, I'm Grant Talbot, Mr. Chambers' assistant. I'll be meeting with you today."

Confused and more than a little annoyed, I stammered, "But what about Chambers? I thought, I mean, we were supposed to …"

"Not to worry," Talbot said, sensing my discomfort. "Mr. Chambers is up to speed on your case. Rest assured, you'll have the full power and resources of the firm at your disposal."

"All right, then," I said.

"Good. Please come with me."

Talbot led me down a long hallway past a maze of offices until we reached a conference area with a table big enough for the Last Supper, with extra seating for the in-laws. The room smelled like Lemon Pledge and money.

"Sit anywhere you'd like," he said, motioning toward the table.

Taking a plush chair at one end, I asked, "Are you sure there's enough room?"

Talbot grinned, showing a mouth full of perfect teeth. "My office is being redecorated," he said. "I hope you don't mind."

"Mind? Hell, I was going to order breakfast."

"Actually, I can offer you bagels or sweet rolls, and coffee."

"Coffee would be great."

Talbot picked up a phone, and less than a minute later, a perky

young lady delivered it steaming hot in a mug tastefully decorated with the firm's corporate logo. She was cute enough to be a
calendar model.

"How do you take it?" she asked. It was all I could do to resist
the obvious comeback.

"Black. Thank you."

She laid down a coaster and gently placed the mug on top of
it.

"Enjoy," she said.

When she left, Talbot said, "I trust you'll like it. It's a special
Sumatran blend we have private labeled. You'll find it full-bodied
yet mild, with just a hint of chicory."

I took a sip. "Very nice," I said, hoping that was the thing to
say. It tasted pretty much like regular 7-Eleven coffee to me.

"Well," said Talbot, opening a lizard-skin briefcase and with-
drawing a yellow legal pad. "Let's get down to business. I've been
briefed, but please tell me in your own words why you're here."

In my own words, I recapped my problems with the embezzlement and the IRS. While I spoke, I noticed Talbot doodling on the
legal pad. Instead of taking notes, he was drawing cartoon faces
and stars and swirls.

Toward the end of my story, I stopped in the middle of a sentence, just to see if he was listening. After about twenty seconds of
silence, he looked up from his pad with a puzzled expression.

"Go on," he said.

"Just wanted to find out if you were really paying attention.
Nice drawings, by the way."

"Oh, these," he said, slightly embarrassed. "They help me focus."

"Well, focus on this!" I erupted. "First, I don't like the idea that
Chambers sent some flunky in his place. Second, I think it's pretty
rude that you're playing Pablo Picasso while I'm trying to tell you
what happened. And third, the coffee's not all that fucking great."
I got up to leave.

Talbot turned a bright crimson, but managed to maintain his
composure. "Please, sit down, Mr. Delaney. I didn't mean to of-
fend you."

Softening a little, I said, "I realize I'm not the most important client in the world. But if your office doesn't want my business, just say the word."

"Please, sit down," he repeated. Reluctantly, I settled back into my chair. "That's better," Talbot said, pulling at the perfect knot in his tie. "I can see you're a man who appreciates the direct approach, so I'll get to the point. You're right, we usually don't bother with low-profile guys like you, especially on such short notice. But this is a personal favor to Dean Cunningham. That's how things get done in this town, so we're going to give you our best effort, just as if you were one of our corporate clients. I'm confident we can get the IRS off your back. It's what we do. The details of your story aren't all that important; they're all variations on a theme, anyway."

He paused and took a breath. "When you leave, I'll call the local field office and find out who's been assigned to you. We'll set up an appointment, I'll represent you, and we'll get this matter settled. Worst-case scenario, we agree to a reasonable payment schedule, probably pennies on the dollar, and they remove the lien. The whole thing takes less time than you'd think, and before you know it, you're back in business. Does that sound like a plan you can live with?"

"That's more like it," I said, feeling somewhat better. "But I have to ask, what's this gonna cost me?"

Talbot didn't blink. "Minimum five thousand dollars."

I did enough blinking for both of us. "Five large," I said. The words caught in my throat. "Fuck me."

Talbot sat there expressionless, like one of those marble statues in front of Caesars Palace. Beneath his impassive stare, I could tell he didn't give a rat's ass whether I ponied up or not. This guy was probably one helluva poker player. I hoped he was as good a lawyer. In that instant, I decided I wanted him on my team.

"Deal," I said. "Where do we go from here?"

Talbot allowed himself just a suggestion of a smile. "I'll need a check today for a thousand dollars. You can pay Julie at the front desk. The rest is due when we settle."

"Can I date it for Monday? I've got a little cash-flow problem."

"Of course."

"Then what happens?"

"I'll contact the IRS. In the meantime, assemble all pertinent financial records, plus police reports and anything else that might corroborate your claims. I'll be in touch shortly."

We shook hands and I turned to go.

"Oh, one more thing," Talbot said.

"Yeah?"

"What's wrong with our coffee?"

11

That weekend, everything went right. Bev made an executive decision and hired the Rolling Blackouts, the classic rock band from L.A. As far as I was concerned, their song selections were dead on: "Mony, Mony," "Devil With the Blue Dress," "Good Lovin'," "Ain't Too Proud to Beg." When I was a kid, I used to bug my Dad to put Zeppelin, Sabbath, and Floyd in the jukebox, but he never did. He said some of it sounded like cats in heat and the rest just made him sick to his stomach. These days, my tastes run to the older stuff. Motown, mostly. The crowd must have agreed, because they stayed late and spent more than usual. With the booze flowing like a flash flood down the Las Vegas Wash, I'd have no trouble "borrowing" the grand to cover my attorney's fees.

I stumbled into my condo Saturday morning about 3, tired but happier than I'd been since the break-in. There were four messages on the machine. The first was from a company offering me a free trip to Fabulous Las Vegas. Not much of a deal, considering I already live here. Maybe it was time for them to update their list.

The next message was from Wally.

"Hey, buddy. Just checking in. Still no trace of that brother-in-law of yours. He's either really smart or really dead. I tried calling you at the bar, but they said you were dancing with some of the local talent. Tell me it ain't so. Later." Click.

Next came Sarah, sounding even more fragile than before.

"Jimmy, I know you're working and I don't want to bother you, so just call when you get a chance and let me know if you've heard anything from your detective friend." It was too late to call now, so I'd have to catch her in the morning. I wondered if it was time to come clean about Owen. Vegas is still a small town in many ways and the word might be getting around. I decided it would be better if she heard it from me.

The last message was from my favorite person in the world. "Hi, Jimmy Daddy, it's me. I lost another tooth and I need to know how much it's worth. Last time, I got a dollar, but I pulled this one out myself because it was just hanging there, so I think I should get two dollars since I had to do all the work. Please call soon, so I can write a letter to the tooth fairy if she doesn't leave enough. Miss you and love you. Bye."

Bye, I said out loud. Love you, too. I'll put in a good word with the fairy.

I collapsed into bed and slept for ten hours straight, more than the total of the entire previous week. If I hadn't gotten up to pee, I'm sure I could have knocked off another hour or two.

I whipped up a light brunch of scrambled eggs and sourdough toast. Then I called Jenny to advise her to hold out for two dollars, and Sarah to arrange a get-together. I got lucky for once; she wasn't home. I left a message on her machine about meeting her for lunch on Monday. Wally was out golfing, according to his wife, and I told her to give him a big "fuck you" from me. Evelyn just laughed; she's the kind of woman my Dad would have called a "right broad," the ultimate compliment.

I'm sure he felt the same way about my Mom, but she died suddenly when I was eight. Sadly, as I get older, my memories of her continue to fade, like the color in an old Polaroid. The aroma of a certain perfume, or the sound of a lilting laugh, have a way of transporting me back in time, where I can reconstruct little snippets of scenes. Other than that, I'm stuck with the family albums, where I may as well be looking at strangers. Some day, a psychiatrist might be able to tell me why I don't remember very much. He might also be able to tell me why the photos seem to be getting younger. I'm sure none of this is normal, but then, what is? I don't think I've ever met a "normal" person in my life.

That night, I had a strange desire to attend the late Mass. I hadn't been to church in months, possibly a year, but recent developments had put a crimp in my self-confidence. A small dose of the old-time religion surely couldn't hurt. Not that I make a habit of praying; when pressed, I'm not even certain I believe in God. But there's something comforting about the rhythms and rituals. Apparently, a lot of folks feel the same way, because stately old St. Joseph's was standing-room only. My mind wandered during the sermon, just as it did when I was a kid. All I can tell you is, it had something to do with sin and redemption and everlasting life. The usual stuff. Sermons are kind of like soap operas. You can miss dozens of episodes, and pick up right where you left off.

All in all, it was a pretty good day. I slept well again and got to work rarin' to go.

My upbeat mood lasted until exactly 11:17 a.m., when I got a call from Grant Talbot, Attorney at Law.

"I've got good news and bad news," he informed me. "Which do you want first?"

"Make it easy on yourself," I said. I've never had the patience for that game.

"Well, the good news is we've got an appointment with Internal Revenue. This Friday at one-thirty. I hope you appreciate it, because I had to pull some righteous strings to bump you to the front of the line."

"I'll be there," I said. "What's the bad news?"

"The agent assigned to your case is Stanford Poon."

I couldn't keep from laughing. It's a lack of maturity thing. "Poon!" I cackled. "That's some fucking name."

Talbot was clearly in no mood for my foolishness. "You'd better get that out of your system right now. Poon's a man we can't afford to piss off."

"I'll be good," I promised, wiping my eyes. "Besides, I'm sure he's heard all the jokes before."

"Yeah, but he's still a touchy son-of-a-bitch. A real hard nose, too. Been with the agency more than fifteen years."

"What the hell kind of name is Poon, anyway?"

"Chinese. He's first generation; his parents are from Hong Kong. Over there, Poon's a common name. Kind of like Jones is to us."

"How do you know so much about this guy?"

"I make it my business to know. I also know his wife's birthday and the names of his kids and what kind of musical instrument he plays."

"I'm glad you're on my side," I said. "See you Friday."

"I'll meet you in the lobby at one-fifteen. Wear something conservative, but not too expensive. And let me do the talking."

"Gladly."

I met Sarah for lunch at Cafe Danielle, a phony French bistro in Summerlin, one of the newer master-planned communities that seem to spring up overnight. She had already grabbed a table in back and waved at me when I came in. Lunch hour was over, so we basically had the place to ourselves. Sarah wore a soft blue turtleneck sweater and jeans, and though she looked like she hadn't been getting much sleep, I was again struck by her resemblance to Joy.

"Jimmy, thanks for meeting me."

"Sure. How're you holding up?"

"All right, I guess. Under the circumstances."

"It's a rough one," I said. "What have you told the girls?"

"That Daddy had to go away for awhile on business. All except Rebecca. She's almost fourteen, and I gave her a watered-down version of the truth. I felt she was entitled to know."

"Is she handling it okay?"

"I think she's in denial, which is just as well. Other than me, the dog seems more depressed than anybody." She ran her fingers through her thick hair and let out a cynical little laugh. "Funny, huh?"

"Hysterical. How's Rachel?"

"She seems okay. I worry because the stress can't be good for her."

Our waitress, a spunky girl probably working her way through college, interrupted the conversation. I wondered if she was looking for a sugar daddy. Then I remembered, that takes money. "Have you folks had a chance to look at the menu?"

"Not yet," I said.

"Would you like to hear the specials?"

"Knock yourself out."

When she left to place our order, I asked Sarah, "So did the cops ever pay you a visit?"

"They won't even come out for something like this. I had to go down to the station and fill out a form. They weren't very optimistic. Thank God for your sergeant friend. At least there's hope." She stared at me intently. "Isn't there?"

I cleared my throat and tried to match her gaze. "There's always hope," I said, trying to sound reassuring. "But there's something I need to tell you." Under the table, my right foot twitched nervously, like it was resting on hot coals. I was glad Sarah couldn't see it.

"What?" she asked in a small voice.

"First, I want you to know that it's all circumstantial evidence at this point. I'm sure there's other explanations."

Her eyes narrowed. "Jimmy, you're scaring me."

"That's the last thing I'm trying to do. Okay, here it is. I just found out that somebody's been embezzling my money from the bar for the last three or four months. All of it. I'm broke, Sarah. But here's the worst part. Owen's the only other person who had access to my accounts. And now he's gone. It doesn't look good."

Despite the tears welling up in her eyes, Sarah said, "That can't be. There must be another explanation. What does your friend think?"

"You don't want to know," I said. "He'd like to send somebody over to your place to ask questions. I've been stalling him up to now."

"Thank you," she said. I noticed she was chewing a small hole in her bottom lip.

Just then, our server arrived with the food. Sensing the tension, she muttered, "Let me know if you need anything," then backed away fast. It came pouring out quickly, sounding like one long word.

Sarah took one look at her plate and pushed it away. "Suddenly, I'm not very hungry."

"Sarah, I have to know. Was Owen in some kind of financial trouble?"

She shook her head. "I don't think so. But he always handled the checkbook. I never had to worry about that sort of thing."

"Me neither," I said, and immediately kicked myself. Sometimes I wish I could control my mouth, but it seems to have a mind of its own.

"Jimmy," Sarah said, "I just don't know about you. Most of the time you seem like such a caring man, and then you turn around and say something that's so hurtful …"

"I'm sorry, that came out wrong, " I apologized. "You don't deserve that. It'll never happen again," I hoped.

"It's okay," she said, but I could tell her feelings were hurt.

"Anyway," I said, "I'm just trying to figure out some kind of motive. Could Owen have been blackmailed?"

Sarah shrugged, a forlorn gesture. "Who knows? An hour ago, I'd say these questions were ridiculous. Now, I feel like anything's possible. You think you know a man after so many years, then something like this happens and knocks you for a loop. I honestly don't know what to think. Tell your friend I'll talk to the police. Just have them call first. I don't want the children there when they come over."

"You got it. Sarah," I added, "I'm very sorry you have to go through all this."

"Well, it's all part of life, isn't it? In a way, this is better."

"How so?"

"Not knowing is the hardest. Now, at least there's the possibility that Owen's alive."

"That's a good way of looking at it."

"But by the time I get through with him," she said, "he'll wish he weren't."

12

I should have gone with my instincts, the ones that told me that Talbot was a dick.

On Thursday, the day before our big appointment with the feds, he called to say he had to reschedule.

"They dropped a new trial in my lap that I can't get out of," he said, by way of explanation. On the speakerphone, his voice sounded like it was coming from the bottom of the Grand Canyon. "I already talked to Poon and he'll squeeze us in next Wednesday at ten-forty-five, so I'll see you there."

On Tuesday, he called again.

"I've got to go out of town for a deposition, so I've had to push our meeting back another week."

"You're killing me," I said, barely keeping my anger under wraps. "Look, this may be just another pain-in-the-ass appointment to you, but it's my livelihood we're talking about here. While you're busy juggling my schedule, I can't get my hands on my money. By the time you're done flying around the country, I'll be selling hot dogs at New York-New York."

Talbot said, "I understand how you feel." In the background, I thought I could hear the sound of pen scratchings on paper. I'm sure he was doodling his ass off.

"I don't think you do," I told him. "So here's what's happening. You go handle all of your important shit, and I'll see Poon by myself. Anything's better than this."

"As your attorney, I'd strongly advise against it."

"Save your breath," I said, "because as of right now, you're not my attorney anymore."

He started to say something else, but I slammed the phone down as hard as I could. It splintered into a hundred pieces. I knew I had just kissed off a thousand bucks, plus another forty for the phone, but at that moment it seemed almost worth it.

The Internal Revenue Service building at Oakey and Decatur looks like a four-story mausoleum. I arrived for my appointment fifteen minutes early, wearing my cheapest suit and clutching a shoebox full of documents. The morning was gray and overcast, like my mood. All of the bravado I'd displayed with Talbot was gone, replaced by a sick feeling in the pit of my stomach and a nervous twitch in my left eye. My plan had been to use the old Delaney charm on this guy, but suddenly that didn't seem like much of a plan at all.

The lobby was painted the same dull institutional green you see in high schools and mental hospitals. After checking the directory on the far wall, I rode the elevator up to the fourth floor, accompanied by a young Hispanic couple who looked even more anxious than I felt, their eyes darting back and forth involuntarily. With only the three of us, the elevator still seemed cramped, and the lingering odor of fear forced me to breathe through my mouth. Part of me hoped the doors would stay shut forever, while the other part was preparing to have a screaming claustrophobic fit. At last, the elevator groaned to a stop, the door crept open, and I found myself in a long linoleum-covered hallway, following the signs to Room 409.

The brass plate on the door said "Stanford Poon, Special Agent, Criminal Investigations Division." Taking a deep breath, I cleared the gunk out of my throat for the hundredth time that day, wiped my palms on my slacks, and knocked.

"Come in," a voice called out. It had a hard metallic edge, like pennies in a coffee can.

The office was utilitarian to the extreme. Just a standard Government-Issue desk, two matching chairs, phone, calculator, and generic computer terminal. No knick-knacks, no pictures of wife and kids, not even a coffee cup. Other than one manila folder and a Bic pen, the desk was as barren as my bank account. The whole place looked like it hadn't existed five minutes before my arrival. Cue the "Twilight Zone" theme. I shuddered and realized I had to take a leak.

Poon stood up from behind his desk and we shook hands. He was a slight man, no taller than five-foot-six, with delicate features, coal black hair, and eyes to match. I figured him to be about my age. His grip was unexpectedly firm and his hand felt calloused, as if he chopped down old-growth trees for a hobby. To my surprise, he wore an impeccably tailored suit, possibly Armani, that had to set him back a couple of g's. Good, I thought. Maybe he's on the take.

"Make yourself comfortable," he said, motioning to the chair. I was sure nobody had ever been comfortable in that chair.

"Thank you," I said, my eye twitching into overdrive. I hoped Poon couldn't see it from where he sat.

Flipping open the file, he said, "Mr. Delaney …"

"Call me Jimmy," I said in my most ingratiating manner.

"Jimmy. And how are you today?"

"Just having fun," I said, testing a smile.

"Good," he said, smiling in return. "I'm certain this won't be nearly as unpleasant as you've been led to believe. There are, unfortunately, many rumors and half-truths about the service, most of which have very little basis in fact."

"I'm relieved," I lied. This was no time to let my guard down.

Poon paused to read a few lines in my file before saying, "Correct me if I'm wrong, but I thought you had representation."

"I beg your pardon?"

"An attorney."

"Oh, right. I, uh, had to let Mr. Talbot go. We had some differences of opinion."

Poon appeared buoyed by the news. "It's just as well," he said. "In my experience, Mr. Talbot is more a hindrance than a help."

"Well, I never had much use for lawyers." Impulsively, I asked, "Do you like lawyer jokes?"

"Who doesn't?"

"Did you hear about the lawyer who was so fat, when he died they couldn't find a coffin big enough? They gave him an enema and buried him in a shoebox."

His laughter seemed genuine, a high-pitched wheeze that sounded like air escaping from a tire. At last, he said, "Here's one for you. If you're stranded on a desert island with Hitler, Sadam Hussein, and a lawyer and you have a gun with only two bullets, what do you do?"

"I give up."

"Shoot the lawyer twice."

"That's a good one," I said. "I'll have to remember that." Hey, we're bonding, I thought. Maybe this Poon's not such a bad dude, after all. Pressing my luck, I said, "Nice suit."

He puffed up like a peacock. "You like it? My uncle's a tailor in Hong Kong. Two hundred dollars, American. People think it's designer."

"Had me fooled."

"If you want, write down your measurements before you go and I'll have one made for you."

"Thanks. That's very nice of you."

"What color and material?"

"Oh, just like yours," I said. This was almost too easy. "You know, this is great. I was hoping we could have a nice chat and settle this like two regular guys."

"That was my hope, as well," he said. He returned his gaze to my file. "Well, let's take a look. According to this, you've been making your payments, but your brother-in-law never mailed them. Instead, he absconded with the funds."

"That's about the size of it. He had power of attorney."

Poon made a sympathetic clicking noise with his tongue. "Most unfortunate," he said. "I suppose you brought a copy of the police report."

"Right here," I said, fumbling around in the cardboard box for a few moments before coming up with the document. I handed it over proudly. Jimmy Delaney was nothing if not prepared.

He examined it and said, "Everything appears to be in order."

Now I was really starting to relax. I could feel my bunched-up shoulders inch their way down to their normal position. Fuck Talbot, I thought. I just saved myself four big ones.

"So," I said boldly, "you can see I'm simply an innocent victim."

Poon's tone changed so rapidly, it gave me a chill. "Innocent, perhaps," he said. "But not entirely blameless."

"What's that supposed to mean?" The words shot out before I could rein them in.

"I mean there's a degree of negligence on your part. You'd have to admit that much, wouldn't you, Jimmy?" This time, I didn't like the way he said my name.

"I suppose I could have been a little more careful," I acknowledged grudgingly. "But I've got a business to run, and Owen's my brother-in-law, for God's sake."

"*Ex*-brother-in-law," Poon corrected. It gave me a start. What the hell was in that file, anyway?

"The point is, I trusted him."

"That's apparent," he said flatly. "There's an ancient Chinese expression you'd do well to remember. 'If you put all your eggs in one basket, watch the basket.'"

Just what I need, I thought. Fortune-cookie philosophy. "So, maybe I'm guilty of bad judgment. You can't throw a guy in jail for that, can you?" Poon sat there for a few seconds longer than necessary, steepling his neatly manicured fingers. "Can you?" I repeated, a little too urgently.

Finally, he said, "Of course not. Who said anything about jail?"

"It's just a figure of speech," I said. Shit, that was weak. How did this conversation go downhill so quickly?

"Before we find ourselves engulfed in speculation, why don't we discuss an actual dollar amount? That sounds reasonable, doesn't it?"

It was a classic sales technique, suckering me in with a series of seemingly innocuous questions. And I was letting him.

"Sure," I said.

Poon stared intently at another page in my file, made some lightning quick entries on his calculator, printed out a sheet of paper, and examined it with satisfaction.

"Based on your estimated tax for the last three quarters, plus interest and penalties, we arrive at a total of fifty-six thousand, four hundred eighty-five dollars and ninety-eight cents—"

"Jesus H. Christ!"

He looked up from the paper disapprovingly, one eyebrow arched in a sinister manner.

"Of course, that's strictly a preliminary number. We won't know the exact amount for a few more days."

"Take your time," I grumbled, sinking into my chair. I felt as if somebody had stuck a pin in my ass and I was deflating at an alarming rate.

Poon seemed not to hear me. He continued, "That's in addition to your regular quarterly payments, which I trust, you'll see to personally from now on. Not to tell you your business, Jimmy, but I believe a more hands-on approach is in order." Beneath the cool professional exterior, I could tell the bastard was clearly enjoying himself. "Do you have any questions?"

"Just one. What kind of payment schedule are we talking about?"

"Oh, I think we can stretch this out over the course of one year. That would be, let's see …" he punched a few more numbers into his calculator, "… roughly four thousand, seven hundred seventy dollars and sixteen cents per month."

"Can't forget the sixteen cents," I said. "Are you sure we can't work something out?"

Poon looked startled. "How do you mean?" he asked, a little too quickly.

The warning lights came on and I backed off before I got into real trouble. "I don't know," I said. "It's something I heard in a movie once."

"Well, I'm afraid not."

Before I could stop myself, I reached into my pocket, pulled out my key chain, and handed it across the desk.

"What's this for?" he asked.

"The keys to the bar, my condo, and my piece-of-shit Mazda. It looks like I won't be needing them anymore."

"Let's not be hasty, Jimmy," Poon said. I wished he'd start calling me Mr. Delaney again, but it was too late now.

"I'm serious," I plowed on. "There's no way I can pay you people that kind of money and keep my doors open."

"My clients say that all the time, but there's usually a solution. What about a second mortgage on your condominium?"

"I'm upside down as it is."

"You can always cash in your investments."

"Other than my Lear Jet and the villa in the South of France, I'm tapped."

He consulted my infernal file, momentarily confused. "I don't see any mention of that in here," he said.

"It's a joke, Poon," I said. "Where's your sense of humor?"

"Believe it or not, we don't know everything. This isn't the KGB."

"No, *they* just torture and kill you."

Poon let that slide. He was probably used to worse from his other "clients." I was starting to hate that term. It's not like I hired the asshole.

"Well," he said, "is there anybody you can talk to about a personal loan?"

"I'll consult my cousin Bill. You know, Bill Gates. Perhaps you've heard of him."

"There's no reason to get snippy."

"Are you kidding me? There's every reason to get snippy. You're gonna put me out of business. Then what do I do?" At that moment, I had an image of Steve Wynn, the casino mastermind, in an Uncle Sam costume. I realized that casino owners and the U.S. government were in the same business—of taking your money, your property, even your hope. At least the casino gave you free drinks.

"Some of our clients have been known to use their credit lines to satisfy their obligation, and then, um, file for debt reorganization."

"You mean max out my MasterCard, then stiff the credit-card company through bankruptcy? That's your fucking suggestion? Well, thanks, but no thanks. You're some piece of work, you know that? Your mother must be very proud."

"Actually, she is. She thinks America is the greatest country in the world, and her son is helping keep it that way. I must say, I agree with her."

"Everybody says that. 'America's the greatest country in the world.' Who's in charge of the ratings, Consumer Reports?"

"It's a known fact," Poon said. He looked so damned smug, I wanted to hit him.

"Not to me, it isn't. I've never been to Canada or Switzerland or Costa Rica. I hear those places are pretty nice."

"It just so happens, they have higher tax structures than we do."

"Big deal. Maybe they get better value for their money. I've read all about those thousand-dollar toilet seats and four-hundred-dollar wrenches our government buys."

"Urban folklore. Regardless, I'm talking about our free-enterprise system. That's what allows people like you to be successful."

"I don't see the free-enterprise system working eighty hours a week at my bar, fifty of them to pay taxes!"

Poon picked up his pen and made a note in my file before saying, "Well, it's obvious we have conflicting points of view. I sincerely hope you have the opportunity to travel some day. I think seeing how the rest of the world lives will increase your appreciation of the United States."

"And I sincerely hope you have to go out and get a real job, instead of sponging off taxpayers like me."

Poon stood suddenly, and for a second I thought he was going to come flying across the desk. Instead, he said, "Our time is up, Mr. Delaney. You'll be hearing from us."

"It's been a slice," I said. Neither of us extended our hand. As I made my way toward the door, I happened to notice the only personal decoration in the entire office. It was a framed eight-by-ten color glossy of Poon, wearing a Hawaiian shirt and playing an electric guitar. "Hmm," I said contemptuously, "I never figured you for a guitar player."

"Just a moment," he said. "I have a question."

"Yeah?" I said, spinning to face him.

"Your bar. Do you have live entertainment?"

"On the weekends. Why do you ask?"

"Jimmy," he said, beaming. "Perhaps we *can* work something out."

13

And that's how Come Monday came to be the new house band at Jimmy D's. "Come Monday," as in Jimmy Buffett's 1974 hit. That's right; Poon and the gang were a Buffett tribute band. Which would have been fine, except for one slight hitch. They refused to play anything recorded after 1977. That ruled out "Margaritaville," "Changes in Attitudes," "Volcano," and anything else people might have actually heard of. When I asked him about it, he said, "It's all about integrity." Pretty ironic, coming from a revenue investigator. His feeling was that Buffett sold out in the late seventies, and Poon wanted no part of it.

"So let me get this straight," I said. "You're a tribute band that won't play the hits."

"We're on a mission."

It was a tough sell, but what choice did I have? In return for booking him into the lounge, Poon stretched my payments over three years and waived some of the stiffer penalties. It was a real eye-opener, finding out how much power one man could wield. Of course, I had to keep it a secret or all bets were off.

"You're doing what?" Bev asked, when I told her I was firing the Rolling Blackouts. "They're the best thing that ever happened to this place. You said so yourself."

"I know," I said sheepishly.

"So what gives?"

"I can't tell you right now. You'll just have to trust me."

Bev had to go along with it, but she forced me to hand them the pink slip myself.

"I'm really sorry," I told Reed, the band's lead singer. He was a likeable guy with an aw-shucks grin and a great set of chops. He could sound like anybody from Burton Cummings to Joe Cocker. "You boys are great," I said. "But something's come up."

His look of disappointment was genuine. "If it's about the money, we'll take a percentage instead," he said. "We were just starting to build a following around here."

"I know, and it's breaking my heart." I handed him a piece of paper. "Here's the name of a friend of mine who owns a bar out in Henderson. I already recommended you, so you're as good as hired."

"Thanks, man," he said. "Anything's better than going back to California. They're running out of electricity over there."

"No place to plug in, huh? Well, you could always go acoustic."

Reed shuddered. "James Taylor ain't exactly my role model."

"How do you feel about Jimmy Buffett?"

"You're kidding, right?"

"Right."

When he opened the door to leave, I could see dollar signs going with him.

Come Monday made their debut that Friday night. Jimmy D's was jammed, mainly because I had failed to mention the change in entertainment. It might have been a tactical error. During the first set, at least a dozen regulars tracked me down. Their opinions ranged from "These guys suck" to "These guys blow." Funny how two opposite words can mean exactly the same thing. By midway through the second set, the crowd had thinned fifty percent. By the end of the third and final set, we were down to a handful of hardcore drunks, an older gent with dual hearing aids, and the band's immediate family. Nobody seemed much interested in four middle-aged Asian guys in genuine imitation Hawaiian shirts, playing tunes so obscure that even Buffett didn't remember them. Bev was giving me the evil eye and the servers kept making snide comments about the lack of tips. I finally offered them $20 each to go home.

"Not so bad for a first night," Poon said after the band had mercifully wrapped up. He was wiping sweat from his forehead and sipping an iced tea. "What'd you think?"

"It was really something."

"How about that steel drum? Nice touch, huh?"

"You just can't get enough steel drum."

"Wait'll the word gets out. You'll have to turn people away."

"I hope you're right."

"Perhaps you could run some advertisements in the local paper."

As diplomatically as possible, I said, "Look, Poon, I can get people in here. The problem is, I can't force them to stay. How about if you mix it up a bit, throw in some Beach Boys and Ventures, maybe a little Jan and Dean?"

Poon recoiled as if he had just broken a tooth on a piece of ice. "No way. They're from different coasts and different eras. That would be like Bruce Springsteen playing Jefferson Airplane."

"Could be interesting," I said.

"For somebody in the entertainment field, you don't know very much, do you?"

"I know when I'm losing my fucking shorts!" I said, pounding my fist on the bar for emphasis. The impact sent a bowl of pretzels flying. Poon flinched slightly, which did my heart good. He had me by the short hairs, but I wanted him to be a little afraid of me.

"Have you ever considered an anger-management workshop?" he asked.

"No, but I was thinking about applying for a job at the post office. It might be fun to waste a few career bureaucrats." Poon's look of displeasure indicated I had scored a direct hit.

"I suppose we could always go back to our previous arrangement," he threatened, reminding me I had no bargaining power in this game.

"That won't be necessary," I backed off. "I'm just venting."

He finished his tea and said, "Come on, I'll introduce you to the other members of the band. They're extremely grateful for the opportunity you've provided."

"They should be."

He led me over to the lounge, where his bandmates were breaking down their equipment.

"This is my kid brother, Yale," Poon said. Yale acknowledged me with a nod and a wave as he wiped down his Stratocaster with a soft cloth. "And my older brother, Duke. He's our drummer."

Unlike his siblings, Duke was big enough to be a sumo wrestler, obviously the product of some recessive gene. When we shook hands, the pressure nearly fused my fingers.

"Easy, big fella," I said. "I might be needing those some day."

"Sorry," he said in the deepest voice I've ever heard. It reminded me of one of those old-timers in a barbershop quartet.

"Duke doesn't know his own strength," Poon said. "He's also hard of hearing, so you'll have to speak up."

"Okay!" I shouted. "Here's a drummer joke. Why do people learn to play drums?"

"Why?" Duke asked.

"So they can hang out with the band."

He laughed like Herman Munster.

"Just out of curiosity," I said, "how come they named you all after colleges?"

"Oh, you picked up on that," Poon said. "Very astute. My father was a fisherman and my mother was a seamstress. Their fondest dream was for us to become educated. They thought the names might help."

"And did they?"

"They helped get our asses kicked when we were in school. All except Duke. But it must have worked, because Yale's a dentist and Duke's a vet."

"Where'd you go wrong?" I asked.

"Nowhere. I'm simply a humble civil servant," he said with a theatrical bow.

"Humble my eye," I said. "And as for that servant part …"

Ignoring me, Poon said, "And this degenerate over here is my cousin, Arnie. He plays the bass."

"I take it you never went to college," I said.

Arnie said, "My folks were going to name me UCLA, but they changed their minds."

"Good call. What do you do for a living?"

"I'm an electrician. I make more than these other guys combined."

I looked at my watch. "Listen, as much fun as this is, it's time to close up shop."

"Thanks for the gig, Mr. Delaney," Duke said, too loud and too low. "We won't let you down."

You already have, I thought. But the big lug sounded so appreciative, I kept my mouth shut.

"See you tomorrow," Poon said.

"Yeah."

"Cheer up," he said. "Things could be worse."

14

Poon was right. Things got worse. But not right away.

The next morning, my spirits were lifted by Jenny's regular Saturday call.

"Hi, Jimmy Daddy. Guess who?"

"Britney Spears?"

"No, silly, it's me."

"That was my next guess. What's going on?"

"I have a question."

"Shoot."

"Am I old enough to say 'hell'?"

In the background, I could hear Joy scream, "That's it, young lady! Go to your room!" There was a brief scuffle for the phone, followed by sobbing and the reverberation of a slamming door. Breathing hard, Joy came on the line and said, "See what happens when I send her to visit you?"

"What, you turn into Mommy Dearest? Put my kid back on the phone."

"I will not. She's being punished. It's time I nipped that potty mouth of hers right in the bud."

"She was just asking a question. It's not like she said, 'Go to hell, Mother.' Which isn't a bad idea, come to think of it."

"Sometimes you make me so mad I could ..."

"Good," I interrupted, "I haven't lost my touch."

Fortunately, years of experience had prepared me for the slam that followed, giving me just enough time to move the receiver a safe distance from my ear. Nothing like a fight with the ex to start your weekend; so much for my lifted spirits. Still, to tell the truth, I looked forward to the on-going squabbles with my ex-wife, because they reminded me why we divorced in the first place. Later, when things calmed down, I'd call Jenny and answer her question. To my way of thinking, she could say 'hell' at ten, 'damn' at twelve, and 'fuck' at fifteen, but only as an adjective. It was better to dole them out, or she'd have nothing to look forward to.

I spent the day giving the condo a long-overdue cleaning, losing myself in the repetitive motions of scrubbing and dusting and vacuuming. It's not my specialty, but it's not all that damned hard, either. There's nothing you can't accomplish with a giant economy-size bottle of Windex and a wad of paper towels. Anything was better than dwelling on my money troubles, my ex-wife, the nooky drought, and that fucking Poon. For the first time in a long time, I dreaded going to work.

That night, the dinner crowd was good. Lots of gamblers and no shortage of sweet young things. But at 9 o'clock, when the band launched into its first number, it was as if gang-bangers had hurled a stink bomb through the window. People couldn't head for the exits fast enough. A half hour later, the place was practically deserted and I had no choice but to pull the plug. Literally.

"What gives?" Poon asked, his unamplified voice echoing off the back wall of the nearly empty lounge.

"This isn't working out," I told him, the extension cord still in hand.

"We had an arrangement," he reminded me.

"Yeah, well, look around you. How many customers do you see? I'll save you the trouble. Three. On a normal Saturday, we're filled to capacity. Two weeks ago, the fire marshal gave me a warning, which is a nice problem to have, in case you were wondering."

By now, the band had me surrounded and for an instant I pictured them stomping me. But Duke just stared at the floor dejectedly, saying, "You could have waited 'til the end of our set."

"Listen, I'm sorry, I really am. I wish to high heaven that you guys were any good. I mean, it's not that you stink. It's just that your song selection's not part of this world. Buffett himself would empty the room if he played this stuff. Don't you know any classic rock?"

Poon was in no mood for constructive criticism.

"You're done, Delaney!" he sputtered. "Put a 'Closed' sign on the door right now, because come Monday, this place is a morgue." He seemed pleased at his little play on words.

"I'll find a way to make the payments," I told him.

"It's too late for that now. I'm putting you on the accelerated program. Do you have any idea what that means?"

"No," I gulped. I didn't like the sound of that one bit.

"It means I'll be needing settlement in full by the end of the month or Jimmy D's goes on the auction block." The way he said "I," it was like it was his money.

"All of it?" I asked, not fully comprehending.

"Every last penny."

"That's less than two weeks," I said, trying to control the panic that was rising in my throat like bile. "You can't do that. I'll go over your head."

"I'll bury you in paperwork. By the time it sees the light of day, you'll be eligible for Social Security. Though I doubt you'll be getting that, either." His cold humorless laugh made me shiver.

While my shell-shocked brain desperately struggled for a reply, Poon's brother Yale said, "Stan, what the hell are you talking about? I thought we got this gig because—"

Poon shot him a dirty look. "Shut up, Yale!"

"But you said—"

"I don't give a fuck what I said!" he exploded. "Just mind your own business."

"This is my business," Yale said quietly, but backed off just the same. Duke and Arnie took in the scene, saying nothing.

"Month end," Poon said, waggling his finger in my face, little drops of spit flying out of the corners of his mouth. "I'll teach you to fuck with the Federal Government!"

I still couldn't think of anything to say. So I socked him. Right in his little button nose. He went down like a sack of shit, twitched twice, and lay motionless.

What the hell, I thought. How much more trouble could I get myself into, anyway?

"Sorry," I told Yale with a shrug.

He shook his head sadly, while Duke picked up his younger brother and flung him over his shoulder.

"Oh, well," Yale said. "If you hadn't done that, I would've."

15

Poon never filed charges. Yale, Duke, and Arnie saw to that. They all agreed that he slipped in the parking lot. So I was off the hook as far as criminal battery was concerned. But I still had less than two weeks to raise fifty grand or lose my business, the one that had meant everything to my father. And to me.

On Monday morning, I locked my office door, lit up an unfiltered Camel for the first time in almost a year, and tried to figure out how to make payroll. I could picture the smoke swirling around in my lungs, filling me with an exquisite calm, like sex after a long layoff. Too bad these'll kill you, I thought. The best things always do.

Despite the tobacco and my good intentions, I couldn't get the numbers to cooperate. The weekend had absolutely destroyed me. People don't realize that weekends in the saloon business are like Christmas to a toy store; it's the only time we turn a profit. I'd have to lay off a few of the marginal employees, stall Nevada Power, and make up some cock-and-bull story about Joy's alimony check. That would go over real big, I knew. But hey, I'd do anything to keep the bar open. Anything, that is, except miss a child-support payment. I'd sell a kidney before letting that happen.

Bev handled lunch hour. Every fifteen minutes or so, she knocked on my door to see if I was still alive.

"Go away!" I yelled. "I'm thinking."

"That's what I'm afraid of. Can I get you something?"

"What are you smoking these days?"

"Winstons. Why?"

"Slide one under the door."

By mid-afternoon, I'd whipped myself into such a frenzy, I almost didn't hear the phone ringing. Finally, the sound registered somewhere in my feverish brain and I lunged for the receiver.

"What?"

It was Wally. "You okay, bud? You don't sound like yourself."

"I'm circling the drain," I told him, relating the Cliff's Notes version of the week's events.

"Ain't that the shits," he said when I finished. "What're you gonna do?"

"The suggestion box is open."

"You know any rich guys you can hit up for a loan?"

"Just you."

"Listen, how'd you like to get out of there for awhile?"

"Love to."

"Meet me at the Foundation Room in forty-five minutes. I've got some info about your ex-brother-in-law you might be interested in."

Both pieces of news surprised me. "The Foundation Room, huh? You're traveling in pretty fast company these days."

"Well, don't be too impressed. Last month, a couple of political hotshots, who will remain nameless, had too much to drink up there and wound up beating the snot out of each other."

"I never read anything about it in the local rags."

"That's the whole point. My boys whisked them away before the media knew what happened. Nobody pressed charges and we managed to keep the whole thing hush-hush. The honchos were so goddamned grateful, they gave me a free lifetime membership. So get your ass over here. We'll have a few brews and come up with Plan B. Take the private elevator across from the main registration desk. I'll be in the Buddha Lounge."

"I'm there."

"Oh, and Jimmy ..."

"What?"

"Wear a fuckin' tie."

I'd always wanted to see the House of Blues Foundation Room, but never found the time or felt like calling in a favor. Occupying the entire top floor of the Mandalay Bay hotel tower, it's a super-private club for Las Vegas' movers and shakers, plus any wannabes who feel like parting with the five-grand annual membership fee.

Something must have been wrong with the city's traffic computers, because I sailed through every perfectly timed green light. Here in Vegas, that's as rare as hitting the Megabucks jackpot. For a wistful instant, I found myself wishing I still owned my 'Vette. But those days are long gone. When you drive a 'Vette, you get the kind of women who are attracted to guys who drive 'Vettes.

As I turned right from Tropicana onto the Strip, the midday sun glinted off the hotel windows, rendering my shades nearly useless. I had to slow to a crawl to avoid rear-ending a Dodge Intrepid with New Mexico plates, whose elderly driver was busy gawking at all the big buildings. Of course, the biggest building on the block was Mandalay Bay, a hulking golden presence looming over the Vegas skyline.

I swung into the parking lot and followed the signs to Valet. There, a clean-cut frat-boy type handed me a claim ticket and said, "Good luck." That's the local equivalent of "Have a nice day," and it's almost as sincere. Still, it's better than "Fuck you," which is what a lot of these guys are really thinking. You can't blame them, really; most of their guests are lousy tippers.

Once inside, I made my way through the throngs of slow-moving tourists to the main registration desk, a marble and wood structure roughly the length of a freeway on-ramp. When I asked for directions, a bellman pointed me to a bank of elevators, one of which was marked by a large sign that read, "Foundation Room."

"May I help you?" an exotic young woman asked me. Her name badge said "Lailani." She wore a stylish black suit and stood behind a podium that blocked the path to the elevator. Our eyes met briefly, and I thought I recognized her from a massage parlor I once frequented.

"My name's Delaney. I have an appointment with Wally ... I mean, Sergeant Walter Zelasko. He's a member."

Unimpressed with my connections, she checked a sheet of paper, then used her house phone to gain final approval. When she hung up, she removed the red-velvet rope from the elevator entrance and said, "Greta will meet you when you reach the top."

"Thanks," I said, hoping to find out if she still did that trick with her feet. But she had already returned to her paperwork.

The trip to the Foundation Room took less than 30 seconds and, except for my ears popping, there was virtually no indication of movement. The doors opened onto a scene that gave new meaning to the term "eclectic." Multi-colored Persian rugs, ornately carved doors that might have been African, rooms that appeared to be gouged out of solid rock, all presided over by statues of gods and goddesses that looked, to my untrained eye, to be Hindu or Moslem or Japanese. If some rich guy decorated his house like this, the men in the white coats would take him to a nice rubber room. But here, the whole mess somehow worked. In a word, it was cool.

"You must be Mr. Delaney," Greta said. She was a six-foot blond with skin as pale and flawless as the stone idol beside her. To her right, the Vegas skyline shone through an enormous picture window. I wasn't sure which was more beautiful.

"Nice place you got here," I said. Not my best material, I had to admit. I was seriously out of practice.

She didn't seem to notice. "Thank you. It's strange, no matter how often I come to work, it never gets old."

"I can understand that. This isn't your normal run-of-the-mill Vegas schlock house."

The comment seemed to please her. "That's true," she said, her eyes dancing. "Now, if you'll follow me, I'll take you to Sergeant Zelasko."

She led me through a labyrinth of meeting rooms and alcoves and dining areas, until we reached a cozy dimly lit cubbyhole.

"Here we are, the Buddha Lounge," she said with a polished hand gesture that reminded me of Vanna White. "Please call me if you need anything."

Taking a shot, I said, "I'd like to call and invite you to dinner."

Greta smiled and the fabulous Strip paled by comparison. "That's so sweet. But I'm seeing somebody at the moment. He plays for the Utah Jazz."

"Oh. Well, if you ever get tired of the fast lane, look me up."

"I might just do that," she said, and waltzed out of my life.

True to its name, the lounge was dominated by a large white Buddha, gazing benignly from a center perch and flanked by two lesser statues, probably yes-men. The person it seemed to be staring at was Sergeant Wally Zelasko, whose burly frame was embedded in an antique oversized sofa that might have been filled with goose down. He tried to stand when he saw me, but the couch held fast.

"Hey, buddy, welcome to my world. Have a seat."

"It doesn't look safe," I said.

"Tell you what; it gives you any trouble, I'll shoot it."

Tentatively, I lowered myself onto the sofa, causing Wally's end to rise slightly. The overall effect was that of two big goofy kids on a seesaw.

"Not bad," I said.

Sliding a bottle of Michelob my way across a glass coffee table, he said, "Not bad? This place is the goods. Just watch out for the bullshit factor. Whatever anybody tells you, divide by three."

"Including you?"

"Especially me. But not today. Listen," he said, getting serious, "how much do you know about Owen?"

"Enough, I guess. He is … was … a halfway-decent accountant. Family man, active in his church, no bad habits. Except for that embezzlement thing. We weren't drinking buddies, but he seemed okay. Obviously, I'm not the best judge of character, but you knew that already. Why, what's up?"

"Well," Wally said, taking a deep breath, "you're not gonna believe it …"

"Try me. After the last few weeks, not much surprises me."

"Okay, get this. Owen and his wife have been married fifteen years. They dated about nine months. Guess what he did before that."

"I have no idea."

"Neither do I."

"What do you mean?"

"I mean the guy wasn't alive. He didn't fucking exist, as far as I can tell. No employment data, no driver's license, no social secu-

rity number, no birth certificate, not even a goddamned permanent record from school."

"I thought that followed you around for a dozen lifetimes."

He cracked a smile and took a sip of beer. "Me too. Anyway,
wherever I turn, I run into a dead end. It's like he fell to Earth from
another planet."

"So what is he, some kind of master criminal?"

"Jimmy, you're not as dumb as you look. That's exactly what
I'm thinking. So I call this guy I know, Bob Stiles, over at the FBI."

I'm sure I looked surprised. "Bobby Stiles? Our second-string
quarterback at Paradise?"

"Yeah, I forgot you knew him."

"All I remember is he almost blew himself up trying to build a
cluster bomb in his garage. He's an FBI agent now?"

"Yeah, they're pretty hard up these days. Don't worry, he's in
research. It's not like he's packing heat and kicking down doors.
Anyway, Stiles does some checking around. When he gets back to
me, he's pretty tight-lipped, so I take him out for a few pops, loosen
him up." He paused. "You owe me fifty bucks, by the way."

"What the hell for?"

"Stiles is not, as they say, a cheap drunk. The cocksucker's
drinkin' Chivas like it's cherry Kool-Aid, and I can't get shit out of
him. Finally, he says three words."

"'I'm gonna puke?'"

"'Witness protection program.'"

It took a second to sink in. When it did, I said, "You're shitting
me."

"Nope. It's all he would say. Probably all he knows. But he's
certain that Owen was living a double life. Something must have
spooked him after all these years, and that's why he ran."

"With all my money. Maybe somebody tipped him off they
were closing in."

"Yeah. Either that, or the FBI extracted him. It's been known to
happen. Like an alien abduction. They probe a few orifices, then
set you up with another new life."

I guzzled my beer, reflecting on Wally's story. Finally, I said,
"You know, there could be a third explanation."

"I'm all ears, Sherlock."

"What if Owen was being blackmailed?"

Wally actually looked impressed. "That would explain the un-authorized withdrawals."

"That's right. And when the money ran out, so did he."

"Well put, my amateur friend. Or ..."

"Or what?"

"Or when the money ran out, so did his life."

"So, we're back to the 'Owen's Dead' theory."

"Possibly."

We both sat there on the too-comfortable couch, thinking. With-out warning, Wally struggled to his feet. "I gotta stretch my legs," he said. "Let me show you something."

"I've seen it," I said. "It's not all that impressive."

"Follow me, smart ass."

We left the lounge and exited through a glass door leading to an outside patio. From there, all of Vegas lay before us like one of those aerial cartoon maps you see in the tourist shops.

"What do you think?" Wally asked proudly, like he owned the place.

"I'll take it. What are we, about forty floors up?"

"Forty-three. Other than the Stratosphere, it's the tallest hotel on the Strip. And, unlike the Stratosphere, it's not listing to the right."

"You sound like some kind of guide."

"I took the tour. It comes with the membership." He was lean-ing against the railing, soaking in the whole scene. Below, I could hear the far-away sounds of the traffic on the Strip, floating up to us muffled and dreamlike. I couldn't stop thinking about Owen. Whether he was dead or not really made no difference, at least as far as Sarah and the girls were concerned. Their lives were going to be damned hard just the same. Suddenly, an image of Sarah, soft and vulnerable, flashed into my brain.

"Well, I've seen enough. Let's go in now," I said.

I must have sounded nervous, because Wally asked, "Afraid of heights, Jimmy?"

"No," I said. "Afraid I might jump."

16

"Delaney residence," Jenny said brightly on the other end of the phone. For a second, I thought I had the wrong number. She sounded so professional.

"Hey, kiddo, it's me."

"Jimmy Daddy!"

"Who taught you to answer the phone like that?" I asked.

"Mommy. She says it's polite."

"She's absolutely right."

"I'm mad at her, though." Her tone changed from happy to pouty in an instant. I could almost see her lower lip sticking out.

"How come?"

"She says I can't have a puppy. My friend Heather has a puppy. It's so cute. His name is Bailey. He's a bagel."

"You mean beagle."

"Yeah. So can I have one?"

"Puppies are a lot of responsibility," I said. "You have to feed them and bathe them and take them for walks, even when you don't feel like it."

"I'll do it, I promise. I want one so bad. Pleeese, can I have one, pleeese?"

"Let me talk to Mommy. I'll do the best I can. But no guarantees."

"What kind of teas?" she asked.

"Guarantees. It means I'm not sure. Lately, I'm not so good at talking people into stuff."

"You can do it, Jimmy Daddy. I know you can." She dropped the receiver. In between the banging, I heard her yell, "Mommy, it's for you!"

"Don't hang up," I told Joy when she came on the line.

"What do you want?"

"When's the last time you talked to your sister?"

"Sarah? A couple of months ago, maybe. We've never been close, you know that. Why, what's the matter?"

When I finished telling her about Owen, she said, "That's unbelievable. Poor Sarah. And the kids. Of course, I'll call."

"I know she could use the moral support."

"Thanks, Jimmy. Sometimes, you're not such a bad guy."

"As long as I'm on a roll, I need a favor. You know, Owen's put me in a pretty tight spot, too. He skipped out with more than thirty grand. Can I be a little late on your check this month?"

"The answer is no."

"Jeez, Joy! Owen didn't pay the fucking taxes. The IRS is gonna seize the bar."

"How long do you need?" she asked icily.

"Two weeks, tops."

After a pause, she said, "You never change, do you?"

"I'm trying." I said. "If you'll just give me half a chance."

"I'd like to, but I can't. I'm having major car trouble. Alternator, regulator, they can't figure it out. I need that money right away."

"Why don't you get your future husband to fix it?"

There was an uncomfortable silence. "There is no future husband. We're not getting married."

"I'm sorry," I said, actually sounding sincere, at least to myself. "What happened?"

"He's nothing but a big mama's boy."

"The old lady didn't like you, huh?"

"According to Roger, she thinks I'm some sort of vixen. Whatever that means."

"It just means that you're a fox. Too good looking. Afraid she'll lose her precious boy to you."

"Forget the flattery. Just send the check on time." Then she hung up. I guess I'd have to pick a better time to ask about the dog.

That night, after hours, I sat alone in the dark, bathed only in the blinking blue and gold light of the bar's neon beer signs. Having finished the last of the good whiskey, I started in on the cheap stuff. It burned like Drano on the way down, but I saw it as a form of penance. After the bonehead decisions I'd made lately, I deserved it.

My thoughts kept returning to the conversation I'd had with Sarah earlier in the day, when I attempted to gently inquire about Owen's past. In a spur-of-the-moment decision, I'd stopped by her house on the way to work. It's a nice-looking blue and white Cape Cod, as out of place in the desert as the pirate ships at Treasure Island.

I parked on the street, so as not to drip oil on her driveway. Before I could reach the door, she was standing there, drying her hands on a dishtowel, looking relieved to see me. I'll put an end to that, I thought glumly.

"Jimmy," she said. "What a nice surprise."

"I hope you don't mind. I was in the neighborhood."

"Not at all. You picked a good time. The kids are in school and the baby's down for her nap. Come in."

We walked through the foyer, past a family room piled high with toys, and into a light and airy kitchen.

"Take a load off," she said, indicating a big wooden chair at the foot of a butcher-block table. "What can I get you? Juice, decaf, Seven-Up? I might even have some lemonade from last night. It's homemade."

"I'm fine," I said.

She pulled out a chair for herself and plopped down at a right angle from where I was sitting. "Tell me some good news."

"I wish I could. Actually, the police have hit a dead end. I was hoping to ask you a few questions."

The smile on her face faded, but her tone was still optimistic. "Go for it."

I admired her pluck. Leaning forward in my chair, I said, "How did you and Owen meet?"

"That's an easy one. I was working at Capricorn Books, that

used bookstore over on D.I. Owen wandered in and started asking questions about some of the older religious volumes, histories
of the Mormons, eyewitness accounts of the journey to Salt Lake,
that sort of thing. Well, our tastes were similar, and we started
talking, and the next thing I know he's inviting me out for frozen
yogurt."

"A regular go-to-hell," I said.

"It was exciting enough for me. He was a good-looking young
man; a little on the shy side, but that just made him more attractive, especially compared to the losers who normally came into
the shop."

"Did he ever talk about the past? Where's he from? Are his
parents still living? Any brothers and sisters?

Like a traffic cop, Sarah held up the palm of one hand. "Slow
down, Kojak."

"Sorry. I didn't mean to get carried away."

"Owen was born in Boise, Idaho. His parents were both killed
in a traffic accident when he was a boy. Something to do with a
jackknifed semi. He was raised by his Aunt Helen, on his mother's
side. I never knew her; she died before Owen and I met. He's an
only child, by the way."

"Isn't that unusual for Mormons?"

"Owen wasn't born into the Church. He met some missionar-
ies when he was in college and converted. He says it changed his
life. Before that, he was a big druggie, from what I understand."

"So you two dated for what, less than a year?"

"Nine months."

"And then what?"

"We eloped on Valentine's Day. Pretty corny, right?"

"I'm not one to talk."

"I thought my folks were going to kill me. So, we had a little
reception a few weeks later and they calmed down."

"Were any of Owen's friends at the reception? The ones from
the old neighborhood?"

"It was too last-minute; nobody could make it."

"But you've met some of them since?"

She frowned. "Well, no, now that you mention it. What's this
all about, anyway?"

I swallowed hard, wishing I had taken her up on that lemonade. With a shot of Jack Daniels. "Here's the thing," I said, struggling to find the right words. "The cops have no record of Owen before the two of you hooked up."

Sarah's body jerked as if she'd touched a live wire. "I don't know what that means," she said in a shaky voice.

"They think he might have taken on a new identity. They're not sure why, but that's the theory."

Sarah's eyes started to tear up. Damn, I thought, I was getting too good at making her cry.

"So," she managed to say, "what you're telling me is, his name might not even be Owen."

"It's possible."

"He might have been a completely different person before we met."

"Yes."

"Then our whole marriage is a lie." She said it defiantly, like she'd come to an important crossroads.

Backpedaling, I said, "Let's not get carried away. It's just speculation at this point. There's no proof."

"But it makes the most sense."

"I'm afraid so."

I could see her mind working, sifting through the possibilities. At length, she said, "Well, this fucking stinks," followed by a sound that was half laugh and half sob. I'd never heard her curse before and it caught me by surprise. "Don't look so shocked," she said. "There's a first time for everything."

"You're entitled," I said. "Listen, as long as I'm prying, how's the money situation? Are you getting by?"

"There's a little cushion in the bank, but it won't last long. Plus, a couple hundred in cash I squirreled away here in the house for our anniversary." She looked like she was going to break down again, but rallied. "I'll have to go back to work soon. I've already spoken to my mother about watching the girls."

I said, "You could come work for me, but somehow I can't see you busting your hump waiting tables. That's a compliment, in case you were wondering." Sarah had enough on her mind; I didn't want to tell her that in all likelihood, I'd be joining her at the employment office. The funny part was, I probably had fewer job skills than she did.

"I think I'd make a great waitress," Sarah said. "Keep me in mind."

Eager to change the subject, I asked, "What about Owen's insurance company? Have you contacted them?"

"His agent's on vacation. The secretary told me Owen had life insurance, but I can't collect until he's declared officially dead. No body, no money. For seven years, anyway."

"Jesus. I hate those guys."

"Me, too. I'm learning all about hate these days." She brushed a piece of imaginary lint from the sleeve of her turtleneck.

"Sometimes, that's what it takes to keep you going. That, and a couple of good friends. I'm not in the best financial shape, but if you need anything at all, just let me know. As long as I can get my hands on some flour and tomato paste, you and the girls will never starve."

At that, she started crying again. She leaned across the table and gave me a hug. It didn't take long to feel the tears soak through my shirt onto my left shoulder.

Now, sitting at the bar hours later, listening to the Beach Boys sing "Don't Worry, Baby" for the forty-seventh time, I couldn't erase that image from my mind. Even after four shots of cheap booze.

While my thoughts were miles away, Pete the homeless guy tapped me on the shoulder. My glass fell to the floor and shattered like a fluorescent bulb.

"For Christ sakes, Pete! How many times have I told you, don't sneak up on people like that!"

For a second, I thought he was going to cry. "I didn't mean to scare you. I'll clean it up."

"Leave it. It's kind of symbolic."

"If you say so," he said, looking more confused than usual.

I got up to grab two more glasses, saying, "Join me for cocktails. I'm out of the good shit, so you'll have to settle for Old Horse Piss."

"Beggars can't be choosers." The line seemed to amuse him. "That's funny, huh?"

"Actually, it is," I said, measuring out his drink.

"Here's to crime," he said. He tilted his head and knocked back the amber liquid, his shaggy gray mane flying wildly.

"To crime," I repeated. "Don't say I didn't warn you."

Pete shuddered, but held out his glass for another. As I refilled it, he asked, "So how ya doin', Jimmy?"

Oddly enough, it was the first time that anyone—Wally, Sarah, Joy, Bev—had asked me that since the break-in. So I told him. "I'm in deep shit. The deepest. If I can't pull fifty large out of my ass by the end of the month, the IRS is gonna close me down."

He shook his head slowly. "That's a lot of money."

"Tell me about it."

We both sat quietly for a few minutes, staring at our respective drinks. Pete drummed his dirty fingers on the bartop, keeping time to a song that only he heard. Finally, his face brightened and he said, "I have an idea. What if you held one of those fundraisers where everybody you know comes and gives you money? You've got a lot of friends, Jimmy. Maybe more than you realize."

I briefly considered the idea, then dismissed it out of hand.

"Charity?" I said. "No way I could do that. Thanks, anyway."

"I wish I had another stock tip for you," he said. "But I'm out of the loop."

"If I'd listened to you back then, I wouldn't be in this jam now. But I thought you were nuts."

"I am nuts," he reminded me. "But that doesn't mean I don't know what I'm talking about."

Years ago, right after Pete added Jimmy D's to his route, he told me to buy Universal Gaming Systems stock at $3. "They're undervalued, their price-to-earnings ratio is excellent, and they've got the market cornered on new technology," he said. Just when I started to take him seriously, he added, "And their slot machines make lots of cool noises." Of course, I thanked him and promptly forgot about it. After all, I'd have to be crazy to take investment advice from a homeless man. Except the last time I checked the newspaper listings, UGS was trading at $58 a share. Just another lost opportunity to add to my growing list of deathbed regrets.

"Well, Pete," I said, "even if you gave me a sure thing, I don't think two weeks is enough time."

"That's true."

We drained our drinks. The whiskey was turning my throat raw, but I didn't care, just as long as it provided a time-out from reality.

"There is one more thing," Pete said. "But you probably won't do it."

"Try me."

He fiddled around in his coat pocket and dug out a Zip-Loc sandwich bag so coated with grime, I couldn't see the contents.

"If you're ever down on your luck, this makes a great wallet," he said.

"I'll make a note."

"I hope I still have it," he said mysteriously.

"What is it, a California lottery ticket?" You never knew with Pete. He could be one of those guys with a million bucks stashed in his bedroll.

"Better."

After another minute, Pete extracted a small object so frayed and brown, it reminded me of a withered leaf pressed between the pages of a dictionary. He held it up proudly, like a prospector with a gold nugget. When he handed it to me, I could tell it was a business card, possibly dating back to the Nixon administration. Making a mental note to wash my hands as soon as Pete left, I gingerly held it between my thumb and forefinger, squinting in the semi-darkness to decipher the writing. On the top, in bold black lettering, it read, "DICE ANGEL," with a little "r" in a circle that signified registered trademark. Underneath were the words, "I will bring you luck at craps," followed by "Ask for Amaris" and a local phone number. My spirits sagged. I tried to give the card back to Pete, but he pushed it away.

"I know you think you're helping, and I really appreciate it," I told him, "but this is just another typical Vegas scam."

"No, it's not," he said firmly. "I know a guy who knows a guy who's seen it work."

"I bet there's a whole team of Dice Angels running around taking suckers to the cleaners. Just like those escort services."

"You have to trust me on this. She's like a good witch or something. Please call her," he pleaded. "I don't want you to lose the bar. It's my favorite stop."

His outburst touched me. "Pete, you're all right. But I gotta know. If she's so goddamned good, why haven't *you* hired her?"

He laughed. "What am I gonna do with money? Money just complicates things. I had money once, and it didn't make me happy. I'm homeless because I want to be. It's a lifestyle choice."

"I can't argue with that logic."

"So you'll give her a call?"

I shook my head. "Pete, let me ask you something. In all the time you've known me, have you ever seen me bet so much as a nickel?"

He sat perfectly still for so long, I thought he was having a seizure. Before I could dial 911, he snapped out of it. "Now that you mention it, no. I haven't."

"Would you like to know why?"

"Sure."

"I used to be a player. Blackjack, mainly. Had a line of credit at all the Station Casinos. The pit bosses knew me, called me Mr. D. But I haven't made a bet in five years."

"How come, Jimmy?"

"It was becoming a problem."

Pete nodded knowingly.

"So that's not an option for me anymore," I continued. "Besides, I'm desperate. And when you're desperate, gambling never works. It's like the cards know."

"But this is dice," he said.

"The dice know, too." Pete looked so disappointed, I had to add, "But thanks for caring." I patted him on the back and watched a fine cloud of dust rise toward the ceiling, making swirling patterns in the neon light.

"Well, just keep the card," he said. "In case you change your mind."

I didn't want to hurt his feelings, so I gently tucked it into my wallet, next to my free-car-wash punch card. That, at least, was worth eight bucks.

"What's on the menu tonight?" Pete asked.

"Wings. But all I have left is kamikaze. Hope you don't mind."

"The hotter the better. Maybe you oughta throw in a couple of beers. Just in case."

After I fixed up Pete's to-go box, he polished off the last of his drink, hoisted his gear and headed for the door.

"Think about that Dice Angel, please!" he called on his way out. "I mean, what have you got to lose?"

17

The registered letter from the IRS came early the next morning.

"What happens if I don't sign for it?" I asked Bill, our long-time mailman, a jowly sad-faced fellow less than a year away from retirement.

He pursed his lips and thought for a moment. "I'm pretty sure they firebomb your place."

The letter wasn't a surprise, but it sickened me, nonetheless.

Buried within the assorted bullshit and legalese was the essential message: Pay us fifty-six thousand and change by the end of the month or we'll take away your sole means of earning a living. And you'll still owe us the balance. It was signed by some regional honcho I'd never heard of. That's when it occurred to me: The feds, or at least Poon, would rather shut me down than keep me around as an on-going source of revenue. With that sort of thinking, I'm sure they'd flunk out of Harvard Business School. But what could you expect from the government? I was sure Jefferson, Franklin, and the rest of those guys were turning in their tombs.

I wadded up the letter into a tight little ball and slam-dunked it into the nearest wastebasket. Then, for good measure, I reared back and drop kicked the basket with all my strength. The crash brought Bev running.

"I don't know what's gotten into you lately," she said, surveying the scene. "You're acting like a jerk."

"Who's acting?"

"See, that smart mouth of yours is exactly what I'm talking about. I know things are bad, but you're not helping matters any. Not with that piss-poor attitude."

"Give it a rest, Bev. I'm under a lot of pressure right now, in case you haven't noticed."

"Noticed?" she shot back, her voice rising a dozen decibels. "How could I not notice? Even the staff wants to know what the hell's going on. You owe them an explanation, don't you think?"

"Bev, I'm tired. I'm running out of hope. I don't owe the staff squat, if you want to know the truth."

She stared at me in silence, fuming. At last, she said quietly, "I'm very disappointed in you, Jimmy." When I didn't respond, she asked, "Do you know who else would be disappointed?"

"No clue." I knew it was coming, but I wasn't about to give her the satisfaction.

"I think you do. Your father."

"That's not fair," I objected, without any enthusiasm.

"It's true. What would he be thinking, watching you get stinking drunk every night, throwing in the towel without putting up a scrap?"

For an instant, I felt like running behind the bar and grabbing the Equalizer, just to shut her up. When the mood passed, I said, "Goddamn it, Bev, the feds have my nuts in a vice. What am I supposed to do?"

"Be a man. Level with the employees. Don't try to do this alone. Maybe somebody's got a bright idea."

"Okay, okay, I'll talk to them soon."

"And for God's sake, lay off the sauce."

"Anything else?" I asked.

"Yeah. And don't start hanging around casinos, looking to get married again."

"Is that all?"

"One more thing. Remember, it's not the end of the world."

Under my breath, I said, "It is for me."

A half hour later, I was still sitting there, staring at the mess from the garbage can strewn all over the floor, when Bev poked her head back in.

"Leave now, before I kill again," I said.

"The staff would like a word with you."

"I've got a word for them."

"Jimmy," she said, "you have to do this."

When my meanest stare had no effect on her, I gave up. "All right, already. But who made you my fucking conscience, anyway?"

"It was put in my job description when your dad hired me."

Like a dead man walking, I shuffled into the lounge, where fifteen or so employees had already assembled. They reminded me of a lynch mob without the rope. Trying for any psychological edge, I stepped up onto the bandstand, flicked on the microphone, tapped it twice, and said, "I'm Jimmy D and I'll be here 'til midnight."

Fifteen pairs of eyes glared at me.

Fine, I thought, I'll go for sympathy. "I'll bet you're wondering what's been going on around here. I'm going to level with you. I've got cancer. The doctor says I have six months to live, max." I punctuated my words with a deep sigh.

"Give it up, Jimmy," said Lisa, one of my old-time waitresses. "Bev already clued us in."

I glowered at Bev and snapped, "Traitor." She telegraphed back a bitter smile. "Okay," I continued, "no more bullshit. I'll make a brief statement and then you can ask questions. Just like the president."

They waited expectantly.

I said, "You've probably heard the rumors floating around here. The truth is, I'm on a bad roll. Owen ran off with all my money, every last cent. So now the I R Fucking S is threatening to sell off Jimmy D's by the end of the month. If you're still hanging around, they'll probably try to sell you, too. It's my fault. I should have paid more attention to the business side of things. Right now, I'm trying to raise fifty grand to keep the doors open, but it doesn't look good. If any of you have that kind of money stashed away in a cookie jar, please see me after the meeting." Scattered coughs and nervous laughter. I paused to scan their worried faces. Finally, I asked, "Questions? Comments? Signs of life?"

A hand shot up. It was Lisa again.

"Should I be looking for another job?"

"I can't tell you what to do. I'm gonna try to keep everything together as long as possible. But you've got to watch out for yourselves. Whatever you decide, there's no hard feelings. Put me down as a reference, I'll give you a glowing recommendation." I pointed at Bev. "All except you."

Mick the bartender asked, "What about loans?"

"Well, I'd like to be able to loan you some money, Mick, but …"

"He's talking about you *getting* a loan and you know it, Big Mouth." My conscience again.

"Oh!" I feigned surprise. "Heh heh. Getting a loan. Sure."

There were a few more chuckles, not nervous this time. Brandi was really smiling at me. Whoa!

"Well," I continued, "I tried to get a loan first thing. But the feds have all my property tied up. Nobody'll touch me."

"There's this guy I know," he said.

"I get the feeling he's not in the Chamber of Commerce."

"The one in Sicily, maybe." When he grinned, his face grew craggier than ever.

"What's the vig?"

"Hundred percent a week."

"I'll keep it in mind," I told him. "Thanks."

"Don't mention it."

"Anybody else?"

"You got any family, Jimmy?" That was K.C., one of my cooks.

"Just a younger brother, Danny. He's career military. We exchange Christmas cards when we think of it."

April, another veteran server, lifted her hand shyly. "Uh, Jimmy, I'd be willing to work just for tips for the next few weeks."

Her offer took me by surprise. While I fumbled for an answer, another voice said, "So would I." It was Andy, a delivery driver.

Within a minute, it was unanimous. Like a ham actor or a cheap politician, I had to hold up my arms to quiet them down.

"I don't deserve your loyalty," I told them. "But I can promise you two things. One, I'm gonna do everything in my power to keep the doors open. And two, I'll find a way to pay you back, each and every one of you."

Spontaneously, they broke into applause.

"Now get back to work," I croaked. The lump in my throat kept me from saying anything else.

18

The buyer from Stinky's Sports Cards and Collectibles said, "It's real."

"Of course it's real," I said. "I was there when he signed it."

We were standing in the bar in front of my framed Al Kaline autographed jersey. The buyer was so young, I was surprised he'd even heard of Kaline.

"I'll give you twelve hundred for it."

"What about the rest of the stuff?"

"That includes the rest of the stuff."

"Go take a flying fuck," I suggested.

I guess he was used to it. "You'll change your mind," he said. "We've got the best prices in town."

After five or six phone calls to other shops, I knew he was right. I also learned a valuable lesson. It doesn't matter what the catalogue says. Stuff is only worth what somebody's willing to pay for it.

Next stop, Murray's Hock Shop on Fremont Street. In Vegas, it seems like there's a Mega Pawn Superstore on every corner, but I prefer the personal approach. I've known Murray since I was a teenager, when my Pop used to drag me around looking for odds and ends to spruce up the bar. I hadn't been to Murray's in years, so I was relieved to see it was still there.

The bell tinkled when I shuffled in. The place seemed a little neater than I remembered, but it still had that familiar musty odor. A bookish man of fifty or so, wearing thick black glasses, looked up from behind the counter as I approached.

"Hi," I said, "is Murray in?"

"He's in Miami."

"Vacation?"

"Retired. Been four or five years now. I'm guessing you're not one of our regulars."

"Well, I used to be."

"Jack Lewis," the man said.

"Jimmy Delaney. Are you the owner?"

He shook his head and snorted. "Just the manager. We're owned by Mega Pawn Superstores. They like to keep their hand in these mom-and-pops for the benefit of their old-time customers, the ones who wouldn't be caught dead in the big places. Target marketing, I think they call it."

"Fooled me," I said.

"It's the way of the world," he said sadly. "But at least they offer medical and dental. So, what can I do you for?"

I unhooked the gold Rolex from my wrist and passed it over to him. He wasn't as impressed as I had hoped.

"Uh huh," he said. "A Yachtmaster, right?"

"You know your watches."

"Well, let's take a look." He reached for a skinny hooked tool and began to pry open the back.

"Whoa," I said. "Is that really necessary?"

"It is if you want cash. It's the only way I can tell if it's the genuine article. I've done this a time or two; I'll be careful, I promise."

It was a moot point, because he'd already popped the watch open.

"What are you looking for?"

"Serial numbers." He removed his glasses and held a jeweler's loupe up to one eye.

"Yeah, they match, all right. You got yourself a real Rolex here."

"What'll you give me for it?"

Lewis continued his examination. "It's in decent condition, but this inscription doesn't help."

"It was a gift from my Dad. For graduating high school."

"A generous guy, your old man."

"He was proud of me."

"Unfortunately, the engraving doesn't mean a thing to anybody but you. It brings down the value a bit."

Lewis was starting to annoy me, but I held my tongue. This was tough enough without pissing him off, which certainly wouldn't get me a better deal. Besides, I told myself, it was all part of the negotiating process.

"You selling or pawning?"

"Pawning. I want it back."

He looked at me dubiously, as if thinking, "That's what they all say." Turning the watch over and over in his bony hands, he finally said, "I'll give you eight hundred for it."

I felt my cheeks grow hot. "That watch cost over ten grand!"

"This ain't retail, pal," he said. "We've got to hold this thing for ninety days. We're assuming all the risk here. Don't you think we're entitled to a little profit?"

I knew he had me by the short and curlies. "Can't you do any better than eight hundred?" I asked. I must have looked pitiful, because his tone became more sympathetic.

"Jimmy, your name's Jimmy, right? Come with me to the back of the store. I want you to see something."

He stepped out from behind the counter, locked the front door, and flipped the sign to "Closed," saying, "I'm not supposed to do this, but you seem like a pretty good guy."

"Thanks."

"But if I'm wrong, just remember I've got a three fifty-seven Smith and Wesson tucked into my waist." He flipped his shirt up to reveal the burnished wood grip.

"You're not wrong," I told him.

I followed him to a beat-up black safe approximately the size of a big-screen TV. Lewis spun the combination so quickly, I couldn't see the numbers if I tried. When he pulled on the handle, the door made a creaking scary-movie sound. Kneeling in front of the safe almost reverently, he pulled out the bottom tray and hoisted it to the counter with a loud grunt. There, on a bed of blue velvet, lay dozens of men's and women's watches, a jumble of gold and silver and chrome, gleaming like pirate's treasure in the store's florescent lights.

"Son of a bitch," I whispered.

"All Rolexes, every single one," Lewis said. "Vegas is the Rolex capital of the world. Guy taps out, it's his ticket home. Except half the time, he tries to get even and winds up staying longer than he planned."

"Like forever."

"You got that right. Listen, I don't want to hurt your feelings, but as you can see, I need another Rolex like I need another hemorrhoid. So eight bills is the best I can do."

"I'll take it," I said numbly.

As he wrote up the ticket, Lewis said, "Remember, the interest is six percent per month."

I said, "I'm in the wrong business."

He just shrugged, then reached in his cash drawer for eight crisp hundreds, snapping them off as he counted like an old-timer at the track.

"Take good care of that watch," I told him on my way out. "I'll be back."

"I believe you," he said, but I don't think he meant it.

Heading for my car, I passed two young girls in Brownie uniforms who, along with an older woman, were setting up a table on the sidewalk between the pawnshop and a souvenir store.

"Would you like to buy some Girl Scout cookies, mister?" one of them asked.

"All I have is a hundred."

She smiled innocently, showing a mouth full of empty spaces that reminded me of Jenny.

"That's okay," she said. "I've got change."

19

The second box of Thin Mints is never as good as the first, especially when you eat them in a row. Luckily, as I sat in my office, I had an unlimited supply of beer to wash them down with. It's one of my favorite combinations, chocolate and beer. Almost as good as cigarettes and pain pills. A little slice of heaven, right in my own backyard.

Every now and then, I'd stare at my left wrist where the Rolex had been. After wearing it more or less continuously for two decades, I felt naked without it. All that remained was the round outline of the watch on my skin, three shades lighter than the surrounding area.

Just once, I glanced upward and said, "Sorry, Pop. I really screwed this one up." Though I listened as hard as I could, I never heard a reply.

On a whim, I took out my wallet and tallied the day's proceeds from selling off my stuff. Two grand. That's what I had to show for my efforts. It's what little pieces of my soul were worth on the open market. At this rate, I'd have my tax bill paid off by, oh, the middle of the century.

When you're drunk, you do strange things. Years ago, I came home three sheets to the wind and decided I needed a shave. I woke up the next day with so much blood on my pillow, the only thing missing was the horse's head. Now, after two boxes of Girl

Scout cookies and I don't know how many beers, I thought it might be a good idea to clean out my wallet. When we were married, Joy used to bug me all the time to get rid of the junk that accumulated in there.

"How can you sit on that lump?" she'd ask.

"I don't even notice it."

That's when she'd go on a rant about bad posture and hip-replacement surgery and God knows what else, and somehow I'd wind up spending the night on the couch. She never realized that my wallet was a security blanket. With all the punch cards and two-for-one coupons in there, if the bottom ever fell out of the bar business, I could always get a free taco.

But in my present inebriated state, none of the contents mattered to me. Joy, though I hated to admit it, was right. All of that junk was just weighing me down. So I began a ruthless house-cleaning project, unburdening myself of my complimentary buffet tickets and video rental cards and half-off topless-club admissions. Even a dry-cleaning claim check from last October hit the wastebasket, now smartly caved in by my size 12 Adidas. The only items worth keeping were my driver's license and pawn claim ticket and … what the hell was this? It looked like the world's rattiest business card. "Dice Angel." Oh yeah, the one from crazy Pete. Sayonara, Dice Angel. Go find yourself another sucker. She was probably dead or in jail, anyway.

But as it floated into the trash can like a piece of brown confetti, Pete's words came back so clearly, I could swear he was in the room behind me. "What have you got to lose?" I jerked around, ready to bellow at him for the umpteenth time, but the office was as empty as my heart. "What have you got to lose?" I heard him say again.

I bent over and snatched the card out of the can, my head swimming from the effort. I lost track of how long I stared at it, watching it come in and out of focus. At last, I glanced up at the clock. It was after two in the morning. "What the fuck," I said to Pete or my Dad or the spider that was busily spinning a web in one corner of the ceiling. "Let's wake her up."

I punched in the number, half expecting a disconnect recording or an all-night escort service. Instead, a machine picked up.

"This is Amaris," the voice said. I'd never heard that name before. It rhymed with glamorous. I'll bet. It continued, "If this is about the Volkswagen, it's a black sixty-seven Beetle with seventy-three thousand original miles. If this is about the kittens, they won't be weaned for another eight weeks. If this is business-related, leave your name and number and I'll call back on the morrow. Ciao!" She actually said that, "On the morrow. Ciao." Her voice was somewhere between scratchy and husky, with an accent that might have been New York or Boston. Definitely back East. Definitely no spring chicken. When the tone sounded, I hesitated for just a moment before saying, "My name is Jimmy. I'm calling about the car." While I was congratulating myself on my smooth handling of the situation, I realized I hadn't left the number. So I called back.

"The ball's in your court," I thought after I hung up. If nothing else, I might become the proud owner of a '67 VW Bug.

20

Two days later, I found myself sitting in a lumpy red booth in the lunchroom of the old Huntridge Pharmacy, on the corner of East Charleston and Maryland Parkway, reluctantly waiting for my Dice Angel. She'd picked the spot, a throwback so authentic, you expected it to be in black and white. The place is an actual relic, not some retro diner that exists only in the mind of corporate America. While I nursed a Coke, I had a chance to soak in the atmosphere, which consisted of a linoleum floor of an undetermined color that might have been green back in the 1940s; real Formica tables flecked with gold and cigarette stains; and a matching countertop accompanied by two dozen stools, standing guard like vinyl mushroom sentries. Any second, I figured, they'd come to life and break into a Disney song and dance. I'd obviously had too much to drink during the past few weeks; the alcohol was turning my mind to oatmeal.

Since every table was a smoking table, I decided to take advantage. I cracked open a new pack of Lucky Strikes, my second since I'd given up quitting. I studied the name on the pack and thought I'd definitely have to be lucky to strike anything other than lung cancer. Lighting up, I noticed the other patrons doing the same. I also realized that I was the youngest person in the joint by at least twenty years. Maybe that's the key to looking young, I thought. Hang around with old people.

Amaris had returned my call the afternoon before.

"It's for you," Bev said, handing me the phone. "Something about a Volkswagen. What in blue blazes are you cooking up now?"

"It's a deal I've been working on. Very hush-hush," I told her. When she leaned in to listen to my conversation, I added, "Take a hike." She nailed me with one of her patented nasty looks, but nevertheless sidled to the other end of the bar.

"Jimmy D," I said.

"You called about the car?" she asked breathlessly. Before I could answer, she proceeded to tell more than anybody needed to know about the damn thing, from its ownership lineage and its repair history to the type of fabric on the re-upholstered seats (sheepskin). I waited impatiently for a break that never came. Finally, I cut her off.

"I don't really care about the car."

In mid-sentence, her stream of words came to a screeching halt. There was an awkward silence before she huffed, "Well, um, why did you call?"

Now it was my turn to be uncomfortable. "I was, uh, just wondering," I stammered, "uh, if you still do that dice thing?"

"Mr. D," she said softly, "we're not getting off to a very good start."

I must have bounced back, because she agreed to meet me. Now she was fifteen minutes late and I was having my doubts. After all I'd been through, how could I possibly even consider going back into the casinos? And with a Dice Angel, no less. Craps wasn't even my game. This had to be the dumbest thing I'd ever heard of. The seconds ticked by and my brain kept chattering away. I looked around for an ice pick to quiet it down.

That's when she breezed into the room, a desert whirlwind in high heels. She was tall, well over six feet, built lithe and lean like an ex-showgirl or ex-dancer. Her clothes were black, a layered thrift-shop hodgepodge of silk and lace, something you might see on a chick singer in a second-rate lounge band. But it was her hair that really stood out. It was too full, too blonde, and too permed, with tight ringlets cascading down her face like some kind of exotic jungle foliage. She did not inspire confidence.

Before I could motion her over, she was already there, sliding into the booth and saying, "I hope you're the guy, because if you're not the guy, I'm going to be *so* embarrassed."

"I'm the guy," I assured her. "Jimmy Delaney."

She tilted her head and studied me a moment. "You don't look like a Jimmy," she said. "More like a James."

I said, "Nobody's called me that in years." A distant memory floated to the surface: My mother was the only one who called me James.

"Well, I will. It'll be our little secret."

She looked better from a distance. Up close, she could have been a hard forty or a soft fifty. Underneath all the makeup, I could see remnants of the attractive woman she once was. But life in Vegas, it seemed, had conspired to rob her of that. Her liquid brown eyes were surrounded by a network of fine lines that looked like the surface streets on a map of L.A. A scattering of vertical creases arched upward from her mouth, the sort of ridges some women get from smoking too many cigarettes. Or sucking too much dick. Her perfume made my eyes water. It smelled like Raid. When she held out her hand, the rings on each finger reminded me of rejects from the Home Shopping Network.

"I'm Amaris," she said. "I guess you figured that out by now."

"I've never heard that name before."

"It's old English. It means 'Child of the Moon.'"

"Of course it does," I said, not surprised at all.

"How old are you?"

"Thirty-nine. Why?"

"Thank God you're not a kid. I'm so tired of kids."

I had no idea what she was talking about, so I let that one pass. She continued, "When's your birthday?"

"Why, you gonna buy me a present?"

"I need to know your sign."

"August seventeenth."

She scrunched up her face. "Oh Christ," she said, "another Leo. My second husband was a Leo."

Suddenly defensive, I asked, "What's wrong with Leos?"

"Honey, the things I could tell you. You just love being the center of attention, don't you?"

"I guess so."

"Well, we'll just have to harness all that energy in a positive way. I want you to start wearing gold and purple."

"Slow down, lady. I haven't hired you yet."

She smiled slyly. "I get the feeling you will. I had a dream about you last night."

This was getting weirder by the second. "How did you know it was me? We've never met."

Her eyes got a far-away look. "Well, it wasn't you, exactly. It was George Clooney. The actor?" She said it like a question.

"I don't look anything like him."

"Somehow, I knew he was you."

Swept up in the moment, I blurted out, "Was I naked?"

"As a matter of fact, you were. But it has nothing to do with sex. In dreams, a lack of clothes implies vulnerability. It's all symbolism."

"Well, I have to admit, I've been pretty vulnerable lately."

She reached into an oversized handbag and produced a red-leather folder with a smiling sun and moon embossed on the cover. They looked like the kind of cartoon figures you see in an old Farmer's Almanac.

"You don't mind if I take notes, do you?"

"Go for it."

"Why don't you tell me why you really called?"

I was getting pretty damned tired of my own story, but I hoped this would be the last time. As I told it, she would interrupt occasionally to ask a question or request clarification on some key point. When I was done, I said, "Bottom line is I need fifty-six thousand by a week from Friday or I lose everything."

She sat there for a few moments, twirling her hair, not saying a word. "Well, that's not the worst thing I've ever heard," she said finally.

"No kidding."

"Not even close."

Before I could press her for details, our waitress, a withered old woman, arrived to take our order.

Amaris said, "I'll have that glorious beef tomato chow mein in the vinegar sauce. And a cup of hot tea. Did you ever get the jasmine I recommended?"

Looking baffled, our waitress said, "We only serve Lipton's."

"Well, you be sure to tell Myrtle she needs to order the jasmine. The customers will simply die for it."

"You shouldn't say that too loud around here," I whispered.

The waitress turned her attention toward me. "What'll you have, dearie?"

"How's that banana cream pie I saw in the case?"

"It's my favorite," she said.

"I'll have that and a cup of coffee."

"Coming right up."

When she left, Amaris said, "Don't you just love this place? It reminds me of the old days."

"Yeah, it's great."

"Now, where were we? Oh, right. Fifty-six thousand dollars. Very doable. I've made that happen before. More, even. But we don't have much time. There's a lot of work to do. A lot of work. First, we've got to—"

I jumped in, "Not to be rude or anything, but before we go any further, I need to find out some things about you."

Hesitantly, she asked, "What kind of things?"

"References, for one. I assume you've got a list of satisfied clients."

"Well, of course," she said, looking relieved.

"Good."

"But, naturally, I can't give out that sort of information. It's very sensitive. My clients like to keep a low profile, as you can well imagine."

"Sure. Then maybe you can tell me about your background. How does somebody get into your line of work?"

"You don't choose it, it chooses you," she said.

"What kind of training do you have? Did you go to school?"

"Life is my school."

This was getting me nowhere. The way she answered questions, I wouldn't hire her as weekend fill-in delivery driver. For one thing, I was sure she'd never pass the drug test.

"Let's try again," I said. "When did you realize you first had the …" I struggled for the word, "… the calling."

I could almost see her mind drift back in time. She said, "Oh, that would have to be nineteen sixty-eight ... no, nineteen sixty-seven. It was right after I married my first husband, Luther. He was a musician, played lead guitar in an Aquarian bluegrass group. The Confederate Yankees, they called themselves. They had one album, but it didn't go anywhere. That boy could flat-out play." She leaned forward and lowered her voice. "But he couldn't do for me like he did for that guitar."

"Uh huh."

"Anyway, they performed all over the world. Wherever somebody would pay them. Except they didn't always get paid. That's how we wound up stranded in Portugal without a nickel to our names. We were camping in some makeshift commune outside of Lisbon, no electricity or running water or anything, and the next day I woke up and Luther was gone. Never saw him again. He left me a present, though."

"What kind of present?"

"The pregnant kind."

"Oh."

"Little Antonio. He's a fine young man now. But I'm getting ahead of myself. So, I split Portugal and bummed around Europe, fell in with a band of gypsies in Romania. Never call them gypsies, by the way. It's an insult. They'll cut your heart out and feed it to the dogs."

"I'll remember that."

"For some reason, they liked me. Next thing I know, they're dying my hair black and teaching me how to tell fortunes. But here's the funny part. I was better at it than they were. Oh sure, they taught me some tricks and techniques, but that's all window dressing. The real stuff, I guess you're born with. I think it freaked them out some, but we were making so much money, it didn't matter. Eventually, I was able to stash away enough to fly back to the States. Standby, of course."

Despite my doubts, I found myself being drawn into her story, picturing the scenes in my mind's eye like an old movie. Just then, our waitress arrived with the food and the spell was broken.

Amaris dug into her plate with great gusto. "This is just the best stuff," she said between massive forkfuls. "You wanna try some?"

"No, thanks. Chow mein doesn't go with cream pie." I took a bite of pie for emphasis. It was as good as it looked.

Disappointed, she said, "You don't know what you're missing."

"Next time. You have some sauce on your mouth."

Wiping it off with her little finger, she continued her saga. "So anyway, back in the good old U. S. of A. I decided I'd had enough of the whole hippie thing. I moved to Boulder, Colorado, enrolled in the university, took a bunch of literature courses, and eventually married my professor. Dewayne. He was the Leo. Very flashy, always had to be the whole show. That was okay, though, because he let me do whatever I pleased. I don't think I every really loved him, but I was terribly fond of him. I also signed up for all the psychology classes I could get my hands on and farmed myself out as a test subject. That's when science confirmed my psychic powers. I blew their little old tests right off the chart."

Now we're getting somewhere, I thought. "And they've got the documentation," I said.

"Who knows? That was thirty years ago. A whole other lifetime. There's a lot more, but I must be boring you."

"Not at all." I glanced at the Coca-Cola clock behind the counter. "Maybe we can finish your bio some other time. Just one more question. How do you do it?"

"Do it?"

"You know, bring me luck."

She swallowed and said, "The short answer is, with charms and incantations. I create a certain positive vibration with sounds and colors and textures. It taps into the power of universal consciousness."

"I see," I said, not seeing at all. "And what's the long answer?"

"Honey," she said, "I don't have the time, and you wouldn't understand."

21

We agreed to meet again the next day, same time, same place. I still had plenty to ask her, but I had to get back to the bar and she had to get to work. Turns out she had a part-time day job as an assistant at a 24-hour colon-cleansing clinic on Polaris. On her way out, she handed me a card for ten percent off and said, "You really need to come see us. Your aura's a mess. It's almost black."

"What's that mean?"

"You're leaking energy all over the place. You haven't been taking care of yourself, have you?"

"I've been preoccupied."

"Well, we could flush those toxins right out of you."

I didn't want to tell her that toxins were the only things holding me together.

Driving back to the bar, I managed to catch every red light along the way. Vegas has the longest red lights in the world. In the summertime, cars overheat and die at every intersection, like enormous animals that never make it to the watering hole. It's the main reason so many locals run the reds. It's also why only tourists floor it as soon as the lights turn green.

When I got back to work, Bev said, "No VW?"

I sailed right past her, saying, "I wouldn't be caught dead in that piece of crap. Did you know the engine's in the trunk?"

She just stood there with her hands on her hips, looking at me like I was crazy. Before she could say anything, I was safely in my office with the door locked. I poured myself a tall glass of toxin and leaned back in my chair. There was a lot to think about.

Amaris was certifiable, there was no question about that. My brain told me to head for the hills. But my gut said take a shot. It wasn't easy to ignore a lifetime of skepticism, but short of robbing a bank, what choice did I have? Like it or not, she was my last chance. And she sure seemed confident in her abilities.

But that didn't mean I had to be an idiot about it. Before leaving the lunchroom, I'd carefully wrapped Amaris' teacup in a napkin and slipped it into my pocket. Just an extra precaution, a small insurance policy for a guy who could certainly use one. Now, heading to our second meeting in as many days, I made a brief detour to deliver the cup to Sergeant Wally Zelasko's office in the Southwest Area Command, a one-story gray cinderblock building on Spring Mountain. The sign in the lobby said, "Check Your Guns," but failed to mention anything about teacups. According to the gal at the front desk, Wally wasn't in (probably at the Foundation Room), so I left it with her, safely protected in a Tupperware bowl. On it, I scribbled a note, "Do Not Open 'Til Xmas. Call Me, Jimmy."

By the time I arrived at the Huntridge, Amaris was already waiting for me. I was disturbed to see that she wore the same outfit as the day before. Either that, or she had a closet full of them.

"Sorry I'm late," I said.

"I just got here myself. I ordered you a chocolate shake. They make them with real ice cream."

"Isn't that bad for me?" I asked.

"Not today."

The shake was smooth and delicious, with just the right amount of syrup. I took such a big swig, it gave me brain freeze.

Sensing my discomfort, Amaris asked, "Are you all right?"

"Yeah, sure, it's worth it. Listen, there's some stuff we didn't get a chance to talk about yesterday."

"I know. What do you want to discuss?"

"Like how much you charge."

She straightened up in her seat and said, "You don't beat around the bush, do you, James?"

"I don't have much time."

"Well, it's quite simple, really. My fee is five hundred dollars plus twenty percent of your winnings."

I said, "That's pretty steep, Amaris. What if I lose?"

"You won't lose."

"But what if I do?"

"The five hundred is a guarantee. It's non-refundable. Of course, you wouldn't owe the twenty percent."

"Very generous. Okay, so let's say I decide to hire you. How does it work, exactly? Do you shoot the dice or do I?"

"You do. I stand behind you, holding my amulets and chanting very softly. The last thing I want is to call attention to myself. It's very behind-the-scenes."

"Which brings up an issue," I said. It was so obvious, I don't know why I didn't think of it till now. "If you can do what you say you can, what the hell do you need me for? Why not just be your own client and make a fortune."

"I can't concentrate when I play on my own. I need a partner."

"Fair enough. But I gotta warn you. You've got your work cut out for you."

She looked mildly surprised. "Why is that, James?"

"I'm not a lucky guy."

"How so?"

"I lose. Every time. Even on my birthday."

She shook her head. "Nobody loses every time."

"I do. That's why I haven't played in years."

I could see she was pondering my last statement. At length, she said, "Is it possible you don't know how to play properly?"

"Not at all. In fact, I'm a walking gambling encyclopedia. Doesn't make any difference. I've had dealers tell me I'm the unluckiest son-of-a-bitch they ever saw. Other times, it's like fishing. They say, 'You shoulda been here yesterday.' I got to the point where, if I heard that one more time, I'd have to kill somebody."

As she had yesterday, Amaris extracted the red folder from her purse. Mumbling to herself, she flipped through the pages until she stopped on one near the end. "I'd like to ask you some questions," she said. "Sort of a gambling pop quiz."

"Sounds like fun."

"Here we go. In blackjack, when do you split aces?"

"Always."

"That's right. When do you split tens?"

"Never. Unless you want the guy on third base to beat the living shit out of you."

"Dealer has an eight up, you've got a soft seventeen. Hit or stand?"

"Hit. It's a freebie."

"Hmm. You never learned to count cards, did you?"

"Nah, too much work. But I can keep track of the aces and tens."

"Okay, let's move on to craps. What are the true odds on six and eight?"

"Six to five. Come on, give me a hard one."

She wrote something in her notebook, then said, "What's considered the best you can do against the expectation?"

"Pass line and full odds, the higher the better."

"What's the house edge on a pass line wager backed by three-times odds?"

"Point-six."

She snapped the book shut and looked at me with a bemused grin. "Very good, James. Obviously, you know the rules. But do you know when to break the rules?"

I had to think about that one. "No," I admitted.

"That's why you have me." She took a triumphant sip of tea, knowing she'd closed the deal.

I stuck out my hand and said, "I guess that makes us partners."

Rather than offering her hand in return, she startled me by saying, "I have three conditions."

Fuck, I thought. The old bait and switch. "Yeah?" I asked. "Lay 'em on me."

"Number one. You must never gamble without me."

"I can do that."

"Number two. You must never lie to me."

"Okay."

"And number three. No sex."

That one caught me off guard. "With anyone? Or just you?"

"Just me."

Before I could stop, I blurted out, "Don't flatter yourself, sister."

She didn't seem to mind. "Then it won't be a problem for you?"

"I think I can control myself."

"Good. Because most of my clients have a habit of falling in love with me. My shrink calls it transference."

"You've got a shrink?" I asked in amazement. "Maybe I should hire him."

"It's a her. Except I don't see her anymore. She fell in love with me, too."

"Oh brother."

"So be on your guard."

"The first sign of any feelings, I'm taking a cold shower."

"That's the spirit."

"So," I said, "now we're partners. Right?" This time, she accepted my handshake to cement our arrangement. Her hand felt smooth and cool in mine. "What happens next?" I wanted to know. "When do I pay you?"

"When the timing's right. How much money do you have on you?"

"You mean now? Why?"

"I thought we'd try your luck."

"Don't you mean our luck?"

"Heavens no," she said. "I need to see you in action. So I know what I'm up against."

I riffled through the bills in my wallet. They were all small. "Looks like about thirty-four dollars."

"Not enough. Can you get your hands on some more?"

"I'd have to go back to the bar." Then it hit me. "Wait a minute. I almost forgot." I stuck my index finger into a secret compartment behind my driver's license and pulled out a piece of paper folded to the size of a postage stamp. "My emergency hundred," I said triumphantly. I held it aloft, examining the heavily creased bill. "Damn, I'll bet I've had this over two years. When I was married, I had to hide money from my wife. This is the only one that survived."

"Far out," Amaris said. "Let's go gambling."

22

We drove to Wild Bill's Gambling Hall, a locals casino out on Boulder Highway. According to legend, or at least the casino's PR department, Wild Bill was a prospector who discovered gold on that very spot. Of course, the only gold they dig up these days comes straight from gamblers' pockets. Amaris sat beside me in the Mazda, her legs folded under in some kind of yoga position, breathing rhythmically and chanting "Om." She'd sold her VW that morning and was now without wheels. An environmental decision, she told me before trancing out. I wondered how her meditations would go over on the public buses. If I knew the Vegas citizenry, nobody would even notice.

From the outside, Wild Bill's looks like Hollywood's idea of a town from the old West. Brightly colored false fronts have been made up to resemble livery stables, saloons, jails, tonsorial parlors, and the like. The image of the mythical Wild Bill is plastered everywhere, his long blonde locks and beard flowing freely like Custer's younger brother. Once, a friend of mine applied for work there and was rejected on the basis of too much facial hair. I guess Wild Bill would have trouble getting a job at his own joint.

Inside, it's just another casino. I picked it because I remembered their blackjack rules being more liberal than most. My Dice Angel notwithstanding, blackjack has always been my game of

choice. Because Amaris wanted to observe me in my natural habi-
tat, I was making all the decisions this day. Pulling into the seven-
story parking structure, I was dismayed to find a space right near
the elevators. In my old gambling days, that was always the kiss
of death. It was like using up all my luck before ever entering the
casino.

I swung into the space and gently nudged her awake, thankfully putting an end to the unrelenting "Oms." They were giving
me a headache.

"We're here," I said.

"Lead the way. This one's all about you."

I circled the casino floor a couple of times before settling on an
empty $5 table near the bar. The dealer, a plump plain-faced woman
in her mid-forties, acted like I was bothering her. Her nametag
was cheerier than she was. "Hi," it announced. "My Name is
Dolores. I'm from Iowa."

"Hello, Dolores from Iowa," I said, flashing my friendliest grin.
"Be honest. Are you all alone because you've been kicking
everyone's ass?"

She shook her head slowly, seeming to tire from the effort. "I
just got here."

Commandeering the stool at third base, on the extreme left
side of the table, I spread out my beat-up old hundred. Dolores
studied it uncertainly.

"It's real," I assured her. "I just had a hard time getting it out
of my kid's piggy bank." She didn't crack a smile. I'm sure she
figured I was telling the truth.

"Changing one hundred!" she blared. The pit boss, a young
business-school type, gave her a barely perceptible nod and she
proceeded to lay a stack of blue and red chips in front of me.

I tossed a $5 chip her way. "Can I get a few singles?" I asked.
She glared at me like I was something she'd scrape off her shoe,
but made change nonetheless. Then she began to shuffle the cards,
smoothly melding the decks together using economical move-
ments. Given the same amount of practice, she might have become a concert pianist. Except the tokes aren't as good.

"Double deck?" I asked her.

"Yep," she said, throwing me the solid yellow card that meant it was time to cut. It slid in easily, about two-thirds of the way.

"Good luck," Dolores said dully.

"I could use it."

I placed a $5 chip in my circle, where Wild Bill's rugged frontier features stared vacantly into the distance. Just outside the circle, I positioned a $1 chip, indicating a bet for the dealer.

I said, "I just want you to know. If I'm winning, you're winning." I was using all my old moves.

The dealer's technique was fast and fluid, just the way I like it. As she delivered my first two cards with effortless snaps of her wrist, I experienced the old familiar gambler's rush, a surge of adrenaline that cleared my mind and focused my concentration. I was surprised how comfortable I felt, how natural it all seemed. It was as though the last five years had never happened, almost as if I'd never left this spot. Behind me and just to my right, I could see Amaris intently watching the action. I hoped she couldn't read my mind.

Unfortunately, my luck picked up right where it had left off. My cards were a jack and a nine, a very good hand against the dealer's up card, a six. After sliding my cards under the chips to signal "stand," she flipped over her hole card to reveal a ten, for a total of sixteen. While I was mentally counting my winnings, Dolores dealt herself a four.

"Twenty," she said, whisking away my chip and hers faster than any sleight-of-hand artist. "Thanks for the bet, sir."

"Don't mention it," I said, thinking if she kept this up, it would be her last. "If I could play like you, I'd own this place."

In response, she dealt the next hand. Dolores had a ten showing, while I had a queen and a three, a real stiff. I had no choice but to hit, which I did by scraping my cards against the table. She hit it too hard, breaking me with a nine.

"Twenty-two," I said. "Story of my life."

My next hand was a twenty. The dealer had a twenty as well, and we pushed.

"Good as a win," I said, giving Amaris a quick wink.

Somehow, I won the next hand. I stood pat on a hard eighteen, and watched as Dolores pulled six cards to bust.

I doubled up on my bet and got a blackjack, winning $15. "Now

we're getting somewhere," I told Dolores, putting $2 out for her to
go along with my $20 bet.

My next hand was an eleven, a perfect double down against
the dealer's five. I stacked four red chips next to my original bet,
plus $2 more for Dolores, and caught a king. My 21 turned out to
be overkill, as the dealer busted her fourteen with a ten. She paid
me $40, plus $4 for herself.

"Hey, this game is easy," I kidded her. "How do they keep this
place open?"

Dolores actually chortled, a cracked sound that reminded me
of the rustling of dry leaves.

I upped my bet to $30, dragging the profit, and increasing her
toke to $5. "Let's keep it going," I said.

My next two cards were a pair of aces, a decent split even
against the dealer's ten. I held my breath while Dolores checked
her hole card for blackjack, which would be an instant loser for
me. She didn't have it, so I laid my aces on the table, adding another $30 to the existing bet, along with an extra $5 for her. My
next card was another ace. At most casinos, that would have been
it. But at Wild Bill's, the rules allow you to resplit the ace, a definite advantage for the player. At least, that's the theory. In every
gambling session, there's one pivotal play that spells the difference between going home a winner and just going home. This was
my play. Giving Amaris a little shrug, I placed a third $30 bet on
the table, and $5 more for the dealer, catching, of all things, a fourth
ace. "What the fuck," I muttered, adding $35 to the existing piles.
That gave me $140 in play, with $19 left in front of me. I fired up a
cigarette in an attempt to stay cool.

Time seemed to slow as Dolores peeled off my next four cards.
They were, in order, a four, a deuce, a five, and another goddamned
deuce. Here's what I had to show for all my hard work: a fifteen, a
thirteen, a sixteen, and a thirteen. Four of the worst hands in the
history of blackjack. My face burned hot and my hands turned
cold, twin sensations known to losers the world over. "Stick a fork
in me, I'm done," I moaned. I was certain she had twenty wired.

But wait! Dolores flipped over her hole card to expose a six.
Now the odds swung back in my favor. If she broke the sixteen, a
very good possibility, I had four winners. I could hear the blood

rushing in my ears as she dealt the next card. It was ... an ace. Fuck! What were the odds of that happening? But there it was. Lady Luck rubbing my nose in it yet again, beating me with a stinking seventeen. Five years or five minutes, nothing had changed. Dolores swept away my chips in one graceful motion, looking almost sad. Then I remembered, she was in for $20.

"I hate losing to seventeen," I said lamely.

"You're not very lucky, are you?"

"Really? What was your first clue?" I took my remaining $19 and pushed it in her direction. "These are for you," I told her. "Hell, I'd just lose them, anyway."

"Thanks, sport. You're all right." She tapped the chips twice on the metal tray, signaling a toke to the pit boss, before dropping them into her shirt pocket.

"See you around," I said.

Turning to go, I noticed Amaris waiting for me. Christ, in all the excitement, I'd almost forgotten about her.

"Pretty impressive, huh?" I asked.

In a serious tone I hadn't heard from her until now, she said, "Let's go to the coffee shop and try to figure out what just happened."

23

"Okay," I asked, "what just happened?" We had flopped into a corner booth at Rosa's Cantina, which, if you believed the menu, was run by the great granddaughter of Wild Bill himself. Just more bullshit from an industry built on the stuff. Amaris ordered her usual tea, while I settled for a cup of decaf. In my present agitated state, the last thing I needed was more stimulation.

Taking a sip of her tea and pronouncing it acceptable, Amaris said, "If I'm to help you, I need to ask some questions."

"Fire away."

"Why did you pick that particular table?"

"It was empty. I like to play alone. That way, some convention bozo from Blowjob, Montana, can't come along and fuck me over."

"No, you can do that just fine on your own," she said.

"I see your point."

"What'd you think of that dealer?" she asked.

"I liked her technique."

Amaris frowned. "She didn't have your best interests at heart."

I thought about this for a few seconds. "I know. That's why I made those bets for her."

"Even so, she was still rooting against you."

"Really? Why would she do that?"

"Her ego was more important to her than money. Couldn't you feel the vibe she sent out? It gave me chills."

"Nah, I just figured she was a zero."

"Winning's hard enough when the dealer's on your side," she explained. "From now on, I'd like to see you play at a full table with friendly people and a happy dealer. It makes a difference."

I didn't see how, but conceded, "It's worth a try."

"And another thing. Put a lid on those negative comments. You sound like a loser."

"Yes, ma'am."

"And use your instincts."

"I don't have any."

"Baloney. Everybody has instincts. Yours are just buried under a pile of fear and pessimism and logic. I'm telling you, James, what you really need is to go on a juice fast, plus a couple of sessions at the colon clinic."

I cringed at the thought. "Nobody's sticking a hose up my ass."

"Typical man," she sniffed dismissively. She rooted around in her bottomless purse, finally plucking out a small baggie. "Well, at the very least, try this."

The contents looked like good dope to me. Not a stem or seed in sight. Making sure hotel security hadn't observed us, I spirited the bag into my pocket. "Now you're talking," I said. "What is it, sinsemilla?"

"*Cascara sagrada.*"

"Is it good shit?"

"In a manner of speaking. It's a laxative. All natural. Take it with unfiltered apple juice and it'll open your root chakra."

"My what? Never mind, I don't even want to know. Did anybody ever tell you you've got an anal fixation?"

Amaris rolled her eyes, but otherwise ignored my comment. "Let's get back to blackjack. Why did you tip the dealer your last chips?"

"Just to say 'fuck it.' It wasn't like I was gonna win anything."

"Can't you see how defeatist that is? As long as you have money, you're still in the game. You need to learn patience, my young friend."

I almost laughed. "Patience, that's a good one. I don't have time for that."

She sighed. "You have nothing but time when you're totally in the moment. We'll have to work on keeping you in the present, not counting your money or worrying about the next hand. Remember, focus on intentions, not results. If you do everything right, the results will take care of themselves."

"Whatever. You're the boss." I was getting tired of all this new-age mumbo jumbo.

And wouldn't you know it? That was right when she said, "Now, pay attention, this is important. When you started to lose, what were you feeling?"

"Is this gonna be on the final?" I asked.

"It's up to you," she said cryptically.

I thought about her question. "I'm not sure," I said. "Like a failure, I guess. It dredged up all the old shit, the reasons I quit in the first place."

"Ah ha!" she exclaimed, "now we're getting somewhere."

"If you say so."

She leaned closer, like a prosecuting attorney moving in for the kill. "And what were those reasons?"

I had to pause a moment to sort out my thoughts. "Well, believe it or not, it wasn't so much about the money." She rolled her eyes again, as if thinking, "Yeah right, buster, tell me another one."

"No, really," I said. "I mean, sure, I hated losing, but money wasn't the main thing. See if this makes sense. Night after night I'm playing, making all the right decisions, and the dealer's kicking my ass, just killing me. Like you saw today. Meanwhile, there's some drunk at the table, the fucker's so juiced he can't see straight, and he's breaking the bank. And I'm thinking, what's wrong with this picture? I'm a decent enough guy, hard worker, a good dad. When's it gonna be my turn? When do I get a magic night? And you know what the answer is? Never. That's why I decided to hang it up."

Amaris' lips were pressed into a thin line. "I sense there's more to it than that," she said. "That might be part of the why, but not all of it. Tell me what happened on the last night you gambled. Is there something you remember from that time? You know, the proverbial straw that broke the camel's hump?"

"Back," I said.

"What?"

"Back. Broke the camel's back. That's how the expression goes."

"Not where I'm from."

"Where's that?" I asked. "Saturn?"

She tilted her head back and laughed, saying, "Nowhere that close," and I couldn't be sure if she was kidding. "Stop changing the subject," she added.

"It's my specialty."

"Well, you're not getting away with it. There's something you haven't told me."

"How could you possibly know that?"

"It's my job to know."

This babe was spooky. I took a deep breath and said, "Okay, you win. The night I quit for good, there's this guy on first base. He's in a wheelchair. I think he's young, but who can tell? He's all shriveled and shrunken and he can barely see over the top of the table. Just a sorry bastard, bags of fluid going in and out of him, the whole nine yards. I'm pulling my usual tank job and meanwhile, this guy can't lose. He cannot lose. He's up maybe ten, twelve grand. And the only thing I can think of is, how come he's got all the luck? You know, jealous of a cripple. It finally just dawned on me. That's why I never made another bet until today."

"That's good," she said. "You saw what it was doing to you."

"Yeah. It only took me fifteen years and a piss pot full of money."

"How much money?"

"All of it. That's the first time I came close to losing the bar."

"Heavy."

"I'm sure it didn't do my marriage any good, either." I could almost see myself do a double take. That last statement was as much an eye-opener for me as it was for her.

"Well," Amaris said, "this is going to be tougher than I thought. Of course, we've got the gambling issue. But we also have to look your hatred of money right in the eye."

"Hold on a second. I don't hate money!"

"Yes you do!" she shot back. "Listen to yourself. Money almost ruined your life. And now you're desperate for it again and it's not there. You hate money, and what's more, money hates you." She paused, taking a final sip of her tea. "This goes very deep,

James. Karmic levels. There are dark forces at work here, I can feel it."

"I have no idea what you're talking about," I said.

Covering her eyes with the palm of her hand, she said, "Something from a previous lifetime is keeping you from winning."

"I don't believe in that crap."

"It doesn't matter," she said. "What you believe or don't believe is beside the point."

"I still don't get it. What's this got to do with changing my luck?"

She peered into my eyes and said, "I can't change your luck until I change you."

In a strange way, she was starting to make sense. Either that, or I was losing my mind. "All right," I said, "let's pretend you're on to something. What the hell can I do about it?"

She took out her big bright orange pen, the one that said "Vegas" in shimmering letters, and jotted down something on a corner of the placemat. Tearing it off and handing it to me, she said in a mischievous tone, "I thought you'd never ask."

24

I stopped by Wally's office on the way home. This time he was in. I found him sitting behind his dilapidated desk, chewing out a fresh-faced subordinate who looked to be just out of the Academy.

"And another thing!" he boomed. "I take my coffee with one lump, not two!"

"Yes, sir!" the recruit said.

"Now beat it, before I write you up."

"Yes, sir!" he repeated. He was so anxious to get out of there, he almost knocked me over.

"Tough day?" I asked.

Wally leaned back in his big swivel chair and clasped his hands behind his neck. "These young guys are killing me," he said. "They don't have a lick of sense."

"Not like us when we were their age."

"Fuckin'-A."

"I'm glad you're in. I thought maybe you'd be at the Foundation Room."

"Shhhh, not so loud," he said, taking a quick peek over his shoulder. "The walls have ears."

"Sorry. Hey, I forgot to ask. How's Evelyn like that place?"

"Beats me. I haven't told her."

"Wally, you're my hero."

"A man's gotta have somewhere to hide. Don't you think?"

"Definitely."

"So, what brings you to our little corner of heaven?"

"Did you get the present I left you?"

"Yeah. After the bomb squad got through with it, there wasn't much left."

For a second, I thought he was serious. Then he let loose with a raucous belly laugh that made the whole room shake. Reaching into his bottom drawer, he removed the baggie. "Don't look so worried, old buddy. I got it right here."

"You didn't open it, did you?"

"I swear, you're becoming a little old woman. Is it Christmas yet?"

"No."

"Okay, then. Now, the question is, what the fuck is it?"

"It's a teacup ..." I started to explain.

"I can see that."

"Jesus, Wally, I think I liked you better when you were walking a beat. This whole sergeant thing's gone to your head. Not to mention your gut and your big lard ass."

"I've killed men for less."

"Stick a sock in it. Okay, there's this woman I met. She's trying to help me save the bar. Kind of a partnership. But I don't know anything about her. Not even her last name or where she lives."

Wally rubbed his tired eyes with a thumb and forefinger. "That's not the Jimmy D I know."

"Well, this Jimmy D is fresh out of options. Don't worry, I'm not doing anything illegal."

"And if you are, I don't want to hear about it."

"I'm just trying not to get scammed. That's why I brought the teacup. It's hers. I thought you could have the lab dust it for prints."

"You don't ask much, do you?"

"It's the last time. I swear."

"Where've I heard that before?"

"From your own pie hole. Every time you come to the bar and beat me out of a free meal."

"Oh, yeah. Well, it'll take a couple of days," he said. "If that meets with your approval."

"It'll have to. But remember, I'm on a short time schedule."

"This broad got a name?" he asked.

"Amaris."

Wally took out a pen and flipped open his little spiral note-book. "Spell that."

"A-m-a-r-i-s."

"What the hell kind of name is that?"

"She says it's old English."

Wally snorted. "Probably an alias."

"She works at a colon-cleansing joint on Polaris, if that's any help."

He scribbled down that piece of information as well. "Sounds like a real winner, this Amaris. I hope to Christ you know what you're doing."

"So do I."

He snapped the notebook shut and looked right at me with his steely cop's stare, probably the same one he uses when he's interrogating a suspect. "Jimmy, you gonna save the bar or what?"

"I'm trying."

"But it's a longshot, right?"

I just shrugged and said, "Let me put it this way. It's farther away than Saturn."

25

Even when they have visitors, locals rarely gamble downtown. Other than the Golden Nugget, the casinos are rank and the parking is tight. The last time I stopped by was back in 1996, right after they opened the Fremont Street Experience. The Experience is downtown's ill-advised attempt to compete with the Strip. Ten casinos teamed up with the city of Las Vegas to build a pedestrian mall covered by a four-block-long canopy. One way or another, they finagled public money by getting it designated as a "park," even though there's not a blade of grass in sight.

According to the brochure, "The $70 million Fremont Street Experience turns up the wattage in downtown every night with spectacular computer generated light and sound shows." What that means is, millions of light bulbs, hundreds of speakers, computer animation, and thousands of gawkers craning their necks to watch the same eight-minute show hour after hour.

According to my second cousin Frank from Grand Rapids, the Experience "is the lamest tackiest waste of time I've ever seen. It's free, and it's still not worth it." He's right. I've been more entertained by a fat kid making hand bunnies with a flashlight.

Now, after all these years, I found myself downtown at 3rd Street and Stewart, looking for the office of one Arnie Gilman, Ph.D. That was the name Amaris had written on the placemat at Rosa's Cantina.

"He's a Doctor of Parapsychology," she explained.

Apparently, this quack was going to hypnotize me and send me back to a previous lifetime, so I could get to the root of my troubles.

"No fucking way," I told her. "This is where I draw the line." I slammed my fist on the table to dramatize my point.

Amaris was unimpressed. "Either you go or you can find yourself another angel," she threatened, and I could tell she meant it.

So, here I was, with less than a week before the IRS seizure, parking in front of a shabby white building that had somehow managed to avoid the wrecking ball. Gilman's office sat sandwiched between a taco stand and an upholstery shop. The windows had been whitewashed over and the glass door was adorned with a jagged diagonal crack slightly smaller than the San Andreas Fault. When I entered, a rusty bell with no clapper fell to the floor with a muffled thud. The waiting room, if you could call it that, was right out of a 1940s' detective movie. Except for a three-legged lime green sofa teetering on a patch of threadbare carpet, it was empty.

I wasn't even sure I was in the right place. I started to go outside to double-check the address when an old man stuck his head out from behind a worn curtain and said, "Are you my three o'clock?"

"Depends. Are you Dr. Gilman?"

"Yes I am, yes I am," he said enthusiastically. "Please, come into my office." He spoke with a slight accent that was probably from some Eastern European country that went belly up before World War II. A spry little man in red Sansabelt slacks, he had a pencil-thin mustache and three strands of hair arranged in a spiral pattern across his pink scalp. I followed him through the curtain into a dark ten-by-ten room, where rickety shelves overflowing with dust and books lined three walls. On the fourth wall was a gallery of framed black-and-white glossy photos, featuring a smiling Dr. Gilman with various dead celebrities. Some, like Jimmy Durante and Larry from the Three Stooges, I recognized. The rest looked vaguely familiar, but impossible to name.

"You like my little hall of fame?"

"Very nice. Who's this?" I asked, pointing to a guy with a trumpet.

"Louis Prima. He was before your time. Maybe you remember his big hit, 'Just a Gigolo.'"

"I thought that was David Lee Roth."

He furrowed his brow. "No, I'm sure it was Prima. I helped him quit smoking. I worked with all the big stars," he said wistfully. "Most of them are gone now. That's what happens when you get to be my age."

"I hope I find out some day."

Out of nowhere, he asked, "How old do you think I am?"

I've been around long enough to know a trap when I see one. I automatically deducted ten years. "I'm bad at this," I said, covering my ass.

"Come on," he urged, "take a guess."

"Sixty, maybe?"

Proudly, he said, "My next birthday, I'll be eighty-three."

I was actually impressed. "You look real good."

"You know the secret to living a long healthy life?"

"Absolutely not."

He winked and said, "Neither do I. All these putzes think they've got it figured out. No drinking, no fatty foods, no sex. That's living? If you do what they say, forty years can seem like forever. Abstinence is for the birds. Just ask any of my ex-wives. We're all still friends, in case you're wondering."

While he rambled, I zeroed in on a diploma hanging next to the photos. It looked like one of those mail-order jobs you see in the back of *Popular Mechanics*. I wasn't even sure there *was* a University of Brooklyn.

"It's real," he said, as if reading my thoughts. "I was the first Doctor of Parapsychology in Las Vegas. That was back when Vegas was nothing but a cow town. Before Howard Hughes and the big corporations ruined everything. In those days, they all knew Arnie Gilman, from Benjamin Siegel to Benny Binion to Jack Benny. All the Bennies." He stopped just long enough to glance at his wristwatch and say, "But enough of that. You're Amaris's friend, right?" Before I could answer, he went on, "A lovely girl, Amaris. You're lucky to have found her. What do you say we get to work?" He motioned to a beat-up brown recliner held together with duct tape and dirt.

"Wait a minute," I said. "How long have you known Amaris?" Maybe I could finally get some information.

He thought for a moment, looking up at the ceiling as if the answer were printed there. "Five or six years," he said. "She sends me some business. Why?"

"I'm just trying to figure her out. You know, see if she's for real."

"My boy, take some advice from an old man. In this town, nothing is what it seems."

"Thanks, Doc," I said, thinking, well, that's a big help. Warily, I lowered myself into the chair and pushed it slowly back, half expecting it to implode like an old Strip hotel. Instead of sending me sprawling, it was surprisingly comfortable.

"Very good, very good," Dr. Gilman said, rubbing his age-spotted hands together. "Tell me, have you ever been hypnotized before?"

"Not that I know of," I said. "Unless it was by my ex."

Gilman chuckled. "That's a different kind of spell entirely."

I said, "Before we get started, I just want you to know that I'm here under duress. I think that's the word, anyway."

He arched one eyebrow and said, "Not a problem. Willingness is not a prerequisite."

"Just so we're on the same page."

"Okay, here's what to expect. It's not like the movies. I can't make you cluck like a chicken or moo like a cow. No farm animals."

"Good. I'm a city boy myself." Despite my misgivings, I was beginning to like this jovial old man.

"All I'm doing is creating a state of deep relaxation, quieting your conscious mind so that you might remember certain things. There's nothing wrong with that, is there?"

"No," I had to agree.

"I'm going to dim the lights now and put on some relaxing music." As he spoke, he reached for a battered album cover and carefully slid out an ancient LP. "Jackie Gleason," he said. "Not many people know he was a fine orchestra leader. He was a client of mine, too. Thanks to yours truly, he lost over a hundred pounds."

With a soft plop, Gilman dropped the album onto the kind of

portable record player I hadn't seen since I was a kid. The scratchy music that came out might have sounded okay to Edison. Briefly, I looked around for the RCA dog.

"Look, Doc, no offense, but that's a little distracting."

He looked hurt, but lifted the needle nonetheless, asking, "How about some nice running water?" He flipped the switch to a miniature fountain balancing precariously on one of the bookshelves. The sound it made reminded me of a toilet that wouldn't shut off.

"Doc," I asked, "would it be all right if we just had peace and quiet? I don't get very much of that."

Again, Gilman's face flushed with disappointment, but he did as I requested. "I think that can be arranged," he said, trying to recapture his cheerful demeanor. "Now, Mr. Uh ..."

"Jimmy."

"Yes, of course. Jimmy. Are you comfortable?"

"Uh huh."

"Excellent. I want you to close your eyes and follow the sound of my voice. Focus on your breathing. In, out, in, out. Slowly and rhythmically. Very good."

His voice was strong, but soothing. I sank further into the recliner, thinking that even if this was a crock of shit, at least I'd get a good nap.

"Now, Jimmy," he continued, "I want you to relax every muscle, every fiber, every tendon. Start at your scalp. You can feel it getting nice and warm, can't you? Experience the warmth as it moves down to your forehead, loosening it, helping it relax. You are becoming so peaceful and calm. Keep breathing, slowly, slowly, ever more slowly. Now the warm feeling is moving into the area behind your eyes, down into your cheeks, your mouth, your neck. As it does, you are falling into a deeper and deeper state of relaxation."

Son-of-a-bitch if I couldn't feel the warmth. My hands and feet tingled with it, a most pleasant sensation. I was looser than I'd been in weeks, maybe months. But hypnotized? No way.

Gilman was still into his spiel. "Feel your toes getting warm, and now your whole body is in a very deep state of relaxation. Now, I want you to imagine yourself walking down a staircase into the depths of your mind. There are ten steps. With each step, feel yourself descend into a deeper, more comfortable state. One … two … three … keep moving downward … downward … six … seven … eight … you're almost there … nine … and ten. You're at the bottom now. You look down a long hallway. On each side of the hallway are doors. Many many doors, all of them closed."

I could see the doors in my mind's eye. I had the stray thought that this guy was better than I expected, but it drifted down the hallway and disappeared.

"You are attracted to one of the doors. It's the door that holds the answer to your questions. All you have to do is open it. You walk toward the door, pulled as if by some magnetic force. I'm going to count to three. When I get to three, you are going to turn the knob and open the door. One …"

I could see my hand reach for the doorknob.

"… two …"

My fingers tightened around it.

"… three."

I opened the door.

He said, "Walk through the door, Jimmy. On the other side is another lifetime. Your lifetime. The one you chose. The one that holds the key to uncovering your deepest secrets, your innermost desires."

I walked through the door.

A voice said, "I want you to look down at yourself and tell me what you're wearing. Start with your shoes."

I looked down and clearly saw my feet. "I'm wearing sandals of some kind," I told the voice.

"Excellent. Now look at your arms and down at your chest. What do you see?"

"A black robe."

"Where are you?"

I looked around. "I'm in a church. It's old, built out of stone and timber. But big. My body aches; it's cold in here. Very damp."

"What do you see? What's happening right now?"

"I'm sitting on a bench behind a huge wooden table at the front of the church. People are lined up to see me. Dozens of them. They're poor, dressed in rags. An old woman is standing before me, holding a small burlap bag. She's untying the knot and dumping something into a plate on the table. It looks like coins."

"Can you hear what she's saying?"

"She's saying, 'Forgive me, Father, it's been a difficult planting season. I'll have more for the Church next time, I swear.'"

"And how do you reply?" the voice asked.

"I say, 'My child, see that you do. You'll never enter the kingdom of heaven with a meager offering such as this.'"

I went on to describe three or four similar encounters with peasants of various ages. Finally, the voice intervened, "Now, move forward in time, all the way to the moment of your death. What do you see?"

"I'm lying in a massive bed in a fancy room. The bed has four posts and a canopy that looks like silk. The sun is shining through a stained-glass window. I'm surrounded by doctors and nurses and clergymen. A young woman is trying to get me to drink something hot out of a bowl. I can't lift my head."

The voice asked, "And how do you feel?"

"Weak. So very weak. I'm shutting my eyes. I just need some rest. Now I don't hear the voices anymore. I'm sinking into the bed, getting smaller and smaller. I can't feel anything. It's as though I'm floating away. There's nothing, nothing, all black. All black."

"What have you learned from this lifetime?" the voice asked. "What lessons have you come away with?"

"I was a holy man, a man of God. But I didn't perform God's work. I lived in wealth and riches while the people starved. I took what little they had for my own selfish desires."

"And with your new awareness, how will you live from now on?"

"I will strive to do what's right. I will put others before myself."

"Then this lifetime you have experienced has not been in vain," the voice assured me. "Now, I want you to count backwards from ten to one. When you reach number one, you will be wide awake and alert, fully present in the here and now, your body and mind completely integrated, with all of your memories intact. Is that understood?"

"Yes." I began to count. When I had finished, I opened my eyes, blinking rapidly to bring the room into focus. Dr. Gilman sat on a straight-back chair looking pleased. Behind him, leaning against a wall with her arms folded, stood a tall woman dressed in purple. As my vision cleared, I recognized her. It was Amaris.

"I didn't hear you come in," I told her. "When did you get here?"

"Sometime around the Middle Ages," she said smiling.

Dr. Gilman asked, "How are you feeling, Jimmy?"

"Good," I said. "Real relaxed. I gotta hand it to you, Doc. That's quite a show you put on."

"You're the show," he said modestly. "I'm nothing more than a facilitator."

"Well, you facilitated like a mother."

Amaris added, "I'd say you had quite a breakthrough, James. Do you feel differently about hypnosis now?"

"Maybe," I said. From the expression on her face, I could tell it wasn't the answer she was expecting.

"Maybe? How can you say that?"

"I have to admit, it was an incredible experience. Extremely realistic. Just like being there, in fact."

Amaris frowned. "So what's the problem?"

"The problem is, it's also a lot like a Robin Hood movie I watched last month on cable."

A subtle look passed between Amaris and Gilman. "I told you he was a hard case," she said with a sigh.

Gilman scooted his chair closer to mine and said, "Can't you see, it doesn't matter?"

"What doesn't matter?" I asked, genuinely confused.

"Whether you relived a scene from a past life or from a motion picture."

"You've lost me, Doc."

"Both are messages from your subconscious mind," he explained. "Out of everything in the universe, why did you choose to replay that particular scene?"

"Your guess is as good as mine."

"Better," Amaris interjected.

Gilman continued, "Because the message was meaningful to you in some way."

"Ta da!" Amaris blared.

"Can't you keep her quiet?" I asked.

He shook his head. "I'm no miracle worker."

"So let me get this straight," I said, trying to wrap my brain around his reasoning. "You're saying I picked that whole drama because it meant something to me?"

"Precisely."

"Like what?"

"Jimmy, only you can answer that. But based on your own words, I'd guess it has to do with coming to terms with your relationship to money, by living an unselfish life. It's the way to repay your karmic debt."

I thought about that for a moment. "Doc, you shoulda been a lawyer."

"And make my parents ashamed? I think not."

Amaris gathered up her big purse, saying, "Arnie, you're still the best."

"That's what I keep telling everybody," he said. Rising from his chair, he stood on tiptoes to kiss Amaris' cheek. "Don't be a stranger," he told her. Turning toward me, he added, "That goes for you, too."

We shook hands warmly. "Thanks for everything, Doc."

"My pleasure, young man."

"Don't forget to pay the good doctor," Amaris instructed.

"How much?"

"One hundred dollars," Gilman said.

Reaching for my wallet, I joked, "Every time we get together, she costs me a C-note."

"That," Amaris announced, "is all about to change."

26

"Nice of you to drop by," Bev said sourly when I got back to Jimmy D's.

"I'm not staying," I told her.

"Where've you been these last few days?" she demanded.

"Aspen, Maui, the Florida Keys. You know, the usual." I was determined not to let her get on my nerves.

"It's good that you're back. Tony's sick. Food poisoning, he thinks."

I let out a long breath. "I told you not to let the help eat here."

"Quit clowning around and get into that kitchen," she ordered, handing me an apron.

"I told you, I'm not staying. I got stuff to do."

"What stuff?"

"Saving the bar kind of stuff."

"Oh," she said. "Well, at least answer your messages." She handed me a thick stack of notepapers.

I shuffled through them on the way to my office. Joy. Jenny. Marco the Miller distributor. Jenny. Some guy from the Health Department. Jenny. Jenny. Jenny. Well, Jenny it was. I hoped to Christ nothing was wrong. My stomach tightened as I punched in the number.

"Joe's Mortuary," Jenny's sweet voice answered. "You stab 'em, we slab 'em."

Too relieved to be angry, I asked, "What happened to 'Delaney residence?'"

"Jimmy Daddy!" she shouted.

"Yeah. Who did you think it was?"

"My friend Andrew. We're playing a game."

"Does Mom know?"

"No. You won't tell, will you?"

"Of course not. But maybe you better cool it on the mortuary stuff, just in case."

"Okay."

"So how come you called me like fifty-thousand times?"

"I have a question," she said.

"Yeah?"

"Do I have to be a vege … a veget … a person who doesn't eat meat?"

"Who says that?"

"Mommy. She says meat's bad, and all she cooks anymore is boring vegetables. And soft white junk with no flavor. I can't like it."

"Tofu? You gotta be kidding me," I said. Joy's pulled some stupid stunts in her time, but this was the topper. "Put her on the phone."

"She's at the store. Probably buying more yucky stuff."

"Who's watching you?"

"Uncle Roger." Hmm, Roger was back in the picture. Maybe he grew some balls, after all.

"And what does Uncle Roger have to say about the soft white junk?"

"He doesn't like it, but he eats it anyway."

Hmm. So much for those balls. What I wanted to say was, tell Mommy that little girls need their protein. And if she doesn't knock off this vegetable crap, I'll report her to social services. But what I actually said was, "Listen, Daddy's going to be busy for a few days, so I won't have a chance to call. But I'll talk to you this week-end. Next week, you can come out for a visit, and we'll eat tons of hamburgers. Would you like that?"

"Yay!!!" she exclaimed.

I could hear the sound of call-waiting click in on Jenny's line.

"I have to go, Jimmy Daddy. It's probably Andrew. Bye. Love you."

"Me, too." But we were already disconnected. Shoved aside for a seven-year-old boy. I guess I'd better get used to it.

Tossing the rest of the messages in the circular file, I turned my attention to the small office safe, extracting nineteen one hundred dollar bills and stuffing them into my wallet. As if I needed a reminder, the weight of it in my back pocket drove home the seriousness of the situation. Before leaving Gilman's office, Amaris had told me the time had come. Apparently, the moon, the planets, and my biorhythms were all lined up just right.

The plan, if you could call it that, was in two parts. Tonight, we were meeting at the Golden Gate, a downtown grind joint built in 1906, which claimed to be Vegas' first casino. I was finding that Amaris liked all things old. Maybe she was at the original ribbon-cutting ceremony. In any event, according to her, $2,000 wasn't enough of a bankroll, so we were going to turn it into $5,000. Pretty risky, but I had made up my mind to simply give up and let her call the shots. I couldn't believe I was doing this. It went against every instinct in me. But maybe my instincts were part of the problem.

"What's the worst thing that can happen?" Amaris had asked me.

"Oh, I don't know. How about, I lose everything."

"Okay. And then what?"

"And then I'll have to get a real job, probably working at somebody else's bar."

"And then what?"

I didn't much care for this game. "Then I'll be so bitter and pissed off I'll kill the first ass wipe that looks at me cross-eyed, and I'll die by lethal injection."

Amaris just stared at me. "You do have quite the imagination, James."

Now, I told Bev, "Gotta run. How much do we have in the cash register?"

"A couple hundred," she said. "Who wants to know?"

"Hand it over," I demanded, holding out an upturned palm.

Bev looked even more unhappy than usual, but did as I instructed. I jammed the wad of small bills into my shirt pocket.

To my surprise, Bev's face softened. "Good luck, Jimmy."

"I'll need it."

"We all need it. Here, take this." She pressed something round and metallic into my hand. Sneaking a peek, I saw it was a St. Christopher's medal, the raised image worn almost completely smooth by age. Something about the gesture touched me. Until Bev added, "I've had it over fifty years and it's never done a goddamned thing for me. I figure it's due."

27

The Golden Gate was nicer than I remembered. It has a homey old-time feel, decorated in brass and dark woods, with photos of turn-of-the-century San Francisco taking up every available inch of wall space. I found Amaris at the Deli, occupying a small table off to one side. Today's outfit was a fake zebra-skin pants suit, so phony that even the folks at PETA wouldn't object to it. It looked ridiculous, even by her standards. For a single shameful instant, I prayed I wouldn't run into anybody I knew. I also prayed that the waves of nausea gripping my insides would stop, or at least subside. What I really needed was a beer. But I knew Amaris would never allow it. She wouldn't even let me have a cigarette. Something about clogging my energy channels.

Pulling up a stool, I said, "I can see why you picked this place."

"It's got good vibes," she said, her face lighting up. "The original hotel opened in February 1906, which makes it a Pisces. Very spiritual and intuitive. You can do a chart for a building just like you can for a person. Did you know that, James?"

"Actually, no."

"We need every little edge. Did you bring your money?"

"Right here." I whipped out my wallet and showed her the bills.

"I'll take my five hundred now," she said. Just like that.

I methodically counted out five Franklins. With the dexterity of a street magician, she scooped them up and deposited them into her purse. Out of the corner of my eye, I noticed a middle-aged polyester-clad couple staring disapprovingly at us.

"Hooker," I said cheerfully, giving them a little wave.

"Why, I never …" the woman trailed off, turning her attention to her shrimp cocktail.

Amaris played along in her usual good-natured manner. "Thank you, James," she purred, just loud enough for the couple to overhear. "I must say, you were outstanding. And so athletic. I almost feel guilty taking your money." She patted my hand.

My laughter loosened the fist that had my guts in a vice grip.

"That's more like it," she said. "This is going to be fun!"

"Yeah, fun," I repeated, though less than enthusiastically.

She glanced at her watch, an over-the-top art-deco thing encrusted with colorful jewels that couldn't possibly be real. "Ready?" she asked.

"Ready as I'll ever be."

"Just follow my lead," she said. "When we get to the table, buy in for five hundred. Get all twenty-five dollar chips. Play the pass line and take double odds. I'll be right behind you, blending in, looking like just another bimbo." The remark shocked me. I'd never given Amaris any credit for self-awareness. Was it possible this was all part of her act?

She continued, "Don't pay attention to me at all, unless I whisper instructions. Then, make your move quickly, before the next roll. Are you with me?"

"Sure." Her business-like approach had a calming effect on me. For the first time, I believed we might actually pull this off.

"Okay," she said. "Have you ever seen *Guys and Dolls*?"

"It was our high school play."

"Well, like Big Jule said, 'Let's shoot crap.'"

I followed her out to the casino floor, her long-legged strides nearly outpacing my own. The actual pit area was so small, it could have been the living room of an eccentric rich uncle. There were two crap tables. The first was empty, the bored crew milling around, shuffling chips and fondling the dice. The second table had a game in progress, although the players were strangely subdued.

"This will do nicely," Amaris said under her breath.

"They're losing their asses," I said in a panicky voice.

"James, you'll just have to trust me."

I slid into a vacant spot on the left side of the table and dropped five bills on the layout. Just then, the stickman, a tall skinny kid who was mostly Adams apple, shouted, "Seven out! Line away! Pay the don'ts and the last come." The players groaned, but they couldn't even muster enough energy to make it convincing. Again, I had to wonder if Amaris knew what she was doing.

"All quarters," I told the dealer, who expertly stacked two piles of green chips in front of me. Silently, I said goodbye to my hundreds as they disappeared into the drop box.

"Comin' out!" the stickman yelled, and my stomach lurched. "New shooter, new direction. Place your bets. Crap, eleven, any seven!"

I plunked a $25 chip on the pass line and absentmindedly rubbed the St. Christopher's medal. A very old man in a too-big driving cap carefully picked two dice from the dish, stacked one on top of the other, tapped them twice on the green felt, and lofted them at a forty-five degree angle toward the other end of the table. They never made it that far.

"Short roll," the stickman said. "Sir, you'll have to throw them a little harder, so they bounce off the wall."

With an indifferent wave of his hand, the geezer made a noise that sounded like "Aahhh!" before picking up the dice and tossing them again. This time they made it all the way down, ricocheting off the back wall before coming to a complete rest.

"Seven!" the stickman said. "Winner, winner, winner! Pass line winner!"

The dealer, an attractive woman in her mid-twenties, placed another green chip beside mine. I glanced at Amaris for instructions, but she appeared to be in a trance of some sort and didn't acknowledge me. Her lips were moving like a lunatic's, but not a sound came out. I shuddered, the way you do when you have to pee, and realized my arms were covered in goose bumps.

I'm on my own, I thought. What a crock. I knew I shouldn't have paid her up front. Well, it was too late now. Playing conservatively wasn't going to get me anywhere, so I doubled my bet for the next roll.

Again, the old fella went through his pre-roll ritual before sending the dice on their way. "Dice are moving! Hands up!" the stickman warned, and an extremely large man in a Hawaiian pineapple shirt just did get his massive paws out of the way.

"Six!" the stickman yelled like a carnival barker, and the dealer on the other side of the table moved the puck to six on the layout. "The point is six!" he repeated. "No field. Bet it hard!"

He must have been a helluva salesman, because the guy next to me said, "Hard six," tossing a couple of dollar tokens toward the dealer and lighting up a cheap cigar.

"Is that a two-way bet sir?" asked the stickman, not so subtly hustling a tip.

"Only if it wins!" laughed the bettor, knowing that if it lost, it wouldn't matter to him or the dealers.

"It's booked," the dealer said with a grin.

Taking double odds to reduce the house edge, I stuck $100 in back of my $50 pass-line action, again peeking over my shoulder at Amaris. She was still in another dimension, conversing with God or the Devil or the Easter bunny, for all I knew. Whoever it was, she must have been doing something right, because I hadn't lost. Yet.

For good measure, I dropped a chip on the come.

My buddy in the plaid cap lobbed the dice again.

"Ten!" the stickman called. "It came easy. Pay the field."

The dealer took my come bet and positioned it on the ten. I laid down two more to back it up.

"There's a man who knows how to play," the dealer said appreciatively, and as I was congratulating myself on my incomparable gambling skills, the shooter rolled a seven.

"Seven out!" the stickman informed us. Just like that, I was down $200.

Immediately, cold sweat formed in a dozen assorted places like ice on a windshield. As I wiped my forehead, a throaty voice whispered, "It's all right."

I nearly jumped out of my skin. Spinning to face Amaris, I sputtered, "Welcome back. I think."

"I never left."

"Well, just so you know, I'm two hundred in the hole."

"You're whining," she scolded.

"I'm entitled."

She repeated, "It's all right. You needed to lose."

"What the hell are you talking about?"

"It's a sacrifice to Lady Luck."

"I've given her enough over the years. How much does the bitch need?"

"This should do it."

I gave her a skeptical look and turned back toward the table, just as the stickman said, "New shooter!" and passed the dice to Mr. Cigar. I put another of my dwindling supply of chips on the pass line. "Comin' out!" the stickman said.

Mr. Cigar hurled the dice with such force, they bounced halfway back across the table, scattering some player's chips in the process. For all his efforts, the dice came up two.

"Craps. Snake eyes," the stickman said, and I was down another $25.

"I thought we were done losing," I said to Amaris.

Instead of answering me directly, she leaned in and whispered, "Bet the eleven."

It's a sucker bet at fifteen to one odds, but I did as I was told. "Twenty-five-dollar yo!" I shouted, tossing the dealer a chip.

"It's a bet," she said, cocking her head and fixing me with a quizzical look. In a joint like this, that was pretty big action on a single prop.

Mr. Cigar threw a change-up this time, the dice making a slow wide arc toward the wall.

"Yo-'leven!" the stickman shouted. I couldn't believe my ears. Tapping his curved stick on the table next to my chip, he instructed, "Pay the man three hundred seventy-five dollars." As if by magic, three black and three green chips appeared in front of me. Suddenly, the world was a wonderful place.

"Same bet, sir?" the dealer asked me.

I looked at Amaris. "Parlay," she mouthed silently.

"All of it?" I asked incredulously. "You're shitting me." She simply shook her head.

"Here goes nothing," I said to no one in particular. Then, to the dealer, I said, "Let it ride."

Pointing to a sign on the table, she said, "Sir, the limit here is $300."

"Oh, sorry," I said. "Press it to the max."

Mr. Cigar gave me a dirty look. "You gonna take all day?" he growled.

"Jealous?" I asked. I was so fucking nervous, the word came out a squeak.

Now, the pit boss was giving me his full attention, staring a hole through me with soulless gray eyes. Like most of his ilk, he was a no-nonsense fuck who acted like I was winning his money. I hated him instantly.

"Dice are moving," the stickman said, and indeed they were. One of the little buggers took a bad hop and landed in the rail in front of Hawaiian Shirt Man.

"Shit," the shooter mumbled.

"Too tall to call!" the stickman announced.

"Same dice," Mr. Cigar insisted, respecting the well-known superstition that new dice will always result in a losing roll.

"Same dice," echoed the stickman, who passed the offending cube back to the shooter. This time, he added a new wrinkle to his routine by blowing into his hand before the roll. When the dice left his hand, I must have forgotten to breathe. Because, after the stickman finally declared "Yo-'leven!" the air literally blasted out of my lungs.

"Lucky bastard!" Mr. Cigar snarled.

"Fuck," the pit boss mouthed under his breath.

"Way to go!" Hawaiian Shirt Man said, clapping his hands excitedly.

"Forty-five hundred right here!" the stickman ordered. The stacks of black chips materializing before me were more beautiful than a thousand sunsets.

"Congratulations, sir," the dealer said. If she noticed the pit boss's dirty look, she didn't let on.

Swiveling around, I kissed Amaris squarely on her over-painted lips. I'm not sure which one of us was more surprised.

"I love this woman!" I announced, suddenly understanding the need for Rule Number Three. Transference, my ass. It was winning that did it, plain and simple. For the first time in my life, greed was giving me a hard-on.

"We gonna shoot craps or what?" Mr. Cigar asked.

Amaris said, "That was sweet, James. Now, tell the nice dealer to take you down."

"We're done?" I asked in disbelief. "I'm just getting warmed up."

"No, you're not," she said patiently, as if speaking to a child. "You've had enough excitement for one day."

"Still up, sir?" the dealer asked.

Disappointed, I told her, "No, take me down."

"About damn time," Mr. Cigar groused.

I'd had my fill of this asshole. Reaching into my pocket, I pulled out a dollar bill and slapped it on his portion of the rail. "Here, buy yourself a box of smokes."

While the rest of the table laughed, Amaris and I headed for the lounge. But not before I tossed a black chip back on the layout, saying, "A little something for the boys. And the lady."

"Thank you, sir!" they all said in unison. This was shaping up to be quite a night.

In the lounge, a young black guy in a gray fedora was playing a honky-tonk rendition of "Kansas City" on, of all things, a concert grand. Taking the last remaining table, I babbled, "That was un-fucking-believable! You're a genius! Look, I'm still shaking!" I held up my hands to prove my point.

"Yes, James, the adrenaline can be quite overpowering."

"You gotta let me have a beer," I pleaded.

"All right. But just one."

I flagged down a cocktail waitress and ordered a draft, while Amaris asked for something called a House of the Rising Sun.

"Never heard of it," our server said.

"Pay attention, dear," Amaris told her. "Write this down if you have to. Orange juice, pineapple juice, grenadine, vodka, triple sec, gin, bitters, and a little more vodka."

The waitress stuck out her tongue and grimaced before leaving to retrieve our drinks.

"There's no such thing, is there?" I asked.

"There is now." She extracted a Kleenex from her well-stocked purse and, without warning, wiped my mouth. "Lipstick," she said, by way of explanation.

Sheepishly, I said, "I got carried away."

"Not to sound full of myself, but it wouldn't be the first time. You know, James money isn't a downer, as you've believed. Just the opposite. It's the ultimate aphrodisiac."

"Yeah," I grinned. "Not bad for five minute's work. Is it always that easy?"

"Oh, heavens no," she said, shaking her head and sending her curls flying. "Not at all."

"Well, how did you know? About the elevens, I mean."

She thought for a moment. "Normally, I hear a voice. Or I see a vision. Or a feeling comes over me."

"So, what happened tonight?"

"All three."

"Wow. I'm impressed."

"Me, too. It's called a confluence. That's how I knew for sure."

"I'll bet that doesn't happen very often," I said.

"Try never. At least, not to me. You're a lucky man, James."

That last comment stopped me cold. "Nobody's ever said that to me before."

"You should try saying it yourself."

"Very funny."

"No, James, I'm serious," she said. "Say it now."

I hemmed and hawed and looked down at the floor, before managing to mumble, "I'm a lucky man." I never felt more self-conscious in my life.

"When you get home, stand in front of the mirror and say it a hundred times. Like you mean it."

"You're the boss."

"After all," she reminded me, "we still have a long way to go."

28

Here's how my life works. Whenever something good happens, something bad is sure to follow. "Waiting for the other shoe to drop," I've heard it called. Probably an expression cooked up by a squashed bug. This time, the shoe dropped harder and faster than usual.

I should have known. On the drive back to Jimmy D's, I couldn't stop counting my money. I had to pull over at least three times to make sure it was real. Even after duking off twenty percent to Amaris, I had more than five grand. More important than that, I had hope.

"What's our next move?" I asked Amaris before we left the Golden Gate.

"I'll need to meditate, light a few candles, and do some astrological calculations. I'll call you tomorrow and let you know. Right now, I'm thinking Thursday."

"Isn't that cutting it a little close?" I asked her. "Friday's my deadline." With all that had happened, I still had doubts. Winning five large was one thing; beating the tables out of fifty was something else, entirely. It was like moving all the way up from Single A to the Major Leagues in one leap.

"It'll be fine," she reassured me.

I waltzed into the bar and threw my arms around Bev, who backed away like I had leprosy. "Ask me how my night was," I said.

She just stood there with her arms folded.

"Come on!" I begged. "Stop being such a spoil sport."

"Okay, I'll bite," she said with obvious distaste. "Just don't make me dance with you. How was your night, Jimmy?"

"You really want to know?" I was having fun messing with her.

She started to walk away. "Forget it. I'm not in the mood."

"Well, since you asked, it was pretty fuckin' great. I made some money. Not enough to keep the doors open, but I'm on the right track."

She stopped and stared at me. "What are you doing, Jimmy? Selling drugs?"

"Oh, come on, you know me better than that."

"Well, I was just trying to figure out why Wally keeps calling. He won't tell me a thing. Other than it's important."

"Wally keeps calling?" I asked stupidly.

"Didn't I just say that? Quit flappin' your yap and find out what he wants. And if you're in trouble, I'm not bailing you out."

"Not even a cake with a file in it?"

"Call, already!" she commanded, pushing me toward my office.

Wally's extension rang and rang. The message system must have been on the fritz. Our tax dollars at work. I was about to hang up when he snarled, "Zelasko."

"Hey, it's me. Jimmy."

"About goddamned time. Where you been?"

"Trying to make a buck. What's up? You've been driving Bev crazy. Which isn't that tough, by the way."

Wally sighed. "I got news, Jimmy."

The way he sounded made my heart sink, but I tried to hide it. "Spill your guts, copper," I said.

"You ever hear of a mob guy named Vincent Toledo?"

"Can't say that I have. Why do you ask?"

"He might've been a little before our time. Toledo was an enforcer out of Chicago in the late seventies, back when we were still chasing cheerleaders. They called him 'Holy' Toledo, 'cause he used to say a prayer before whacking his victims. A real nut job. Worked directly under Nicholas 'Nicky the Fixer' Ferraro, who was in line to become the boss of the Kansas City mob until he got sent away on murder one for three consecutive life terms."

"This is all very interesting," I told Wally, "but what's it got to do with anything?"

He said, "I'm getting there. The point is, Ferraro gets a permanent vacation in maximum security, thanks to some timely testimony by one Vincent Toledo, who in turn disappears and is never heard from again."

"And they all lived unhappily ever after?"

"Not necessarily."

"Huh?"

"A few days ago, Toledo turns up dead in a fleabag hotel outside of Laughlin. Two shots with a small caliber pistol to the base of the skull."

"I'm guessing it's not a suicide."

"You shoulda been a cop," Wally said. "It's a classic mob hit. Do you see where I'm heading with this?"

"At the risk of sounding dumber than usual, why don't you tell me."

"Let me know if I'm going too fast for you. They transport the body up to County, run the usual charming procedures, fingerprints, dental records, the whole enchilada. And guess what they find out?"

All at once, I knew. "Owen!" I gasped. "Toledo was Owen. Or the other way around."

"Bingo."

"But that's impossible. Owen looked about as Italian as Florence Henderson."

"The feds popped for big-time plastic surgery. Plus, kindly old Doc Randolph, the coroner, says he dyed his hair."

"Jesus." Then, "Oh, shit! Does Sarah know?"

I could almost see Wally shaking his head. "We just found out ourselves. I was hoping you'd tell her. We need her to come to the Coroner's Office tomorrow and provide positive ID. We're about ninety-nine point nine percent sure, but this will ice it. No pun intended."

"I hate this shit," I said. "But we'll be there."

"Good. Oh, one other thing. The lab sent back the results on that teacup you gave me."

The teacup. I'd practically forgotten about it. "Yeah?" I asked, not even sure I wanted to know. "Is it bad?"

Wally snorted, "It ain't good. That's some little hustler you got yourself involved with."

I felt my knees buckle. "What do you mean?"

"Listen, buddy, I gotta get back to work. I'll fax over her rap sheet. How much paper you got in the machine?"

I glanced at the fax. "About five or six pages."

"You better add more."

29

I'd never been to the morgue before. When you run a restaurant, it's not on your regular route. I don't know about other cities, but our morgue is conveniently located just around the block from County General Hospital. Based on rumors I've heard, the hospital should ship their patients directly to the morgue, bypassing all that messy, negligent, medical care. It's more efficient that way.

I told Sarah just enough to get her into my car. On the ride over, neither of us said much. Whenever we made an attempt, the conversation died out mid-sentence, leaving what would have been an uncomfortable silence if we'd cared about such things. Mainly, Sarah sat very still, her eyes glued straight ahead, her hands folded loosely in her lap. I, on the other hand, clutched the steering wheel with so much force, I lost the feeling in my fingers.

When I made the appointment, I spoke to an assistant medical examiner who identified himself simply as Dr. Bob. He instructed me to drive to the back of the red-brick one-story building and ring the bell at the employee's entrance, which would allow us to avoid the wait in the lobby. I parked in the rear next to a dumpster whose lid was thankfully closed. No need to see what these people routinely tossed out. Taking Sarah's sub-zero hand, I led her to the metal door and sounded the bell. Its earsplitting shriek was noisier than any fire-truck siren and even more unexpected. Loud enough to wake the dead. For the hundredth time that morning, I thought Sarah might faint. But she was a strong and determined woman. Her resolve kept her marching forward like an infantry grunt on point, praying that each tentative step would not be the one that finds the landmine.

The door inched open and a monotone voice asked, "Mr. Delaney? Mrs. Johnson?"

"That's us," I said.

"Right on time, I see. I'm Dr. Bob. Please come in." He was a sallow emaciated man who might have been mistaken for one of his stiffs if he stopped moving long enough.

Sarah and I crept through the door into another world. The first thing you notice is the stench. Lingering just beneath the caustic aroma of disinfectant is a rotting presence so tangible, you taste it before you smell it.

"Oh my," Sarah gasped, and this time, I had to prop her up before she hit the gray tile floor.

Apologetically, Dr. Bob said, "I should have warned you about the odor. We're so used to it, we sometimes forget."

If I ever get to that point, I thought, just kill me and throw me on the pile.

"May I offer both of you masks?" he continued.

"Please," I said. He reached into the pocket of his lab coat and handed us each a green surgical mask. I helped Sarah attach hers before putting on mine.

"Follow me," Bob instructed.

Through the mask, I said to Sarah, "Are you sure you want to do this?"

"I have to," she replied, her voice muffled and weak.

Hand in hand, we trudged down the glazed tile hallway, past a half-eaten box of Winchell's donuts resting near a container marked "Medical Waste." I hoped the staff could tell the difference. Rounding a corner, we almost ran into a gurney, one of three stacked up like planes at McCarran.

"Look straight ahead," I advised Sarah, making out the contours of bodies under sheets. I was beginning to understand why this particular stop wasn't listed in the Vegas guidebooks. Not following my own advice, I glanced through a window to see a corpse splayed open like a catfish. If you could forget it was once a human being, the whole scene was actually pretty interesting.

At the end of the hall, Bob ushered us into another gray-tile room that was even colder than my own flesh. Shiny stainless-steel vaults lined the walls like oversized safety-deposit boxes.

"Are you ready to view the deceased?" Bob asked.

As Sarah nodded, gripping my hand tighter, Bob tugged on the handle. The tray slid out noiselessly. Without another word, he drew back the sheet to reveal the lifeless face of Owen Johnson.

Turning away, Sarah whispered, "It's him." A solitary tear trickled down her pale cheek and disappeared behind her mask.

"I'll just need you to sign this form."

"Give us a minute," I told the doc. Then, to Sarah, I said, "I'm so sorry."

"Thank you," she said.

"If there's anything I can do … anything you need …"

"I know."

She didn't say a word on the drive home. Finally, as I pulled into her driveway, she turned to me and said, "I'll be okay. I have to be, for the children."

"You're a brave lady."

"I have to keep remembering, that wasn't Owen back there. The Owen I know died the day he disappeared."

"That's a good way of looking at it."

"The truth is," she said, " I'm not sure he ever really lived."

30

"I'm glad you called," Amaris said. "I need to speak with you."

Coldly, I replied, "What a coincidence. I need to speak with you, too."

As usual, I let her pick the spot. This time, it was the Denny's on East Fremont, across from the old Showboat Hotel, recently renamed the Castaways. In Vegas, hotel names never get discarded for good; they just get recycled. I suppose Denny's was on Amaris's regular bus route. Or maybe today's horoscope had advised her to eat crap.

I strode past the slot machines in the waiting area, past the hostess with the phone glued to her ear, and into the dining room. Amaris was in a big booth next to the kitchen, her notebooks and papers spread out in front of her, intently scribbling something on a napkin. She didn't look up when I slid into the booth.

"Hi, Mabel," I said.

If I shocked her, she hid it well. Calmly and deliberately, she raised her head and peered directly into my eyes, saying, "My my, James, we've been a busy boy, haven't we?"

"Not as busy as you."

"So," she said, "I guess you're going first. Tell me what you've learned."

With a shaky hand, I pulled some folded up papers from my breast pocket. Squinting under the harsh lights, I took a deep breath and read, "Your name is Mabel Brown, a.k.a. Jade Green, a.k.a.

Cindy Merrywell, a.k.a.Amaris Dupree. Born January fourteenth, nineteen forty-two, in Hoboken, New Jersey—"

"I look good for my age, don't I?" she interrupted.

Ignoring her, I continued, "First arrest at the age of thirteen for shoplifting. Dropped out of school in the tenth grade. Lived in a series of foster homes and juvenile facilities until sixteen, at which time you ran away for good. Here, the personal info becomes sketchy …"

"I'd be happy to fill in the blanks for you."

"That's not necessary. I can pretty much trace you by your arrest record. Buffalo, nineteen sixty, pick pocketing."

"Attempted pick pocketing," she corrected. "I wasn't very good."

"Apparently. Milwaukee, nineteen sixty-one, passing bad checks. You weren't very good at that either. Indianapolis, nineteen sixty-two, forgery. Youngstown, nineteen sixty-three, bad checks again. Tulsa, nineteen sixty-four, fraud. Rapid City, nineteen sixty-five, possession of a controlled substance. Man, you hit all the hot spots, didn't you?"

She said, "Sometimes a young lady can't afford to be choosy."

"Nothing in sixty-six or sixty-seven. You take some time off?"

"I told you, I was living abroad."

"Yeah, whatever. You told me a lot of things. Anyway, now we skip to the swingin' seventies, and you're up to some new tricks here in fabulous Las Vegas. Prostitution, prostitution, prostitution. And, oh yes, prostitution. What'd you do, become a specialist?"

Amaris just shook her head. I was starting to feel just a tiny bit guilty. But these things needed to come out in the open. I wasn't quite sure what I was so angry about. Maybe I did know, but not why I was angry with *her*.

I concluded, "So, what do you have to say for yourself?"

She kept cool. No tears, no hysterics, just a look of profound sorrow. In a weary voice, she said at last, "To begin with, James, I shouldn't have to defend or explain myself to you. You're just a client and I've lived up to my end of the bargain. But since you've gone to all the trouble to dig up my background, I'll answer your question. All of those things you mentioned took place a very long time ago. Do you see any arrests after nineteen seventy-nine?"

I shuffled through the sheets of paper. "No," I admitted.

"And while you're looking," she said, "how many convictions do you find?"

Again, I consulted my records. "Looks like two. Big deal. You had good attorneys."

"They were all public defenders."

"Oh," I gulped.

"I was young, okay? I made some mistakes. I've had a hard life. Does it say anything in your precious police report about how I went to UNLV and got a degree in philosophy?"

Now it was my turn to shake my head.

She asked, "And does it mention how I ran cocktails and drove a cab and danced in a lot of third-rate shows to provide for my son? And how he turned out to be a successful businessman and husband and father?"

"No," I said quietly. There was no doubt about it: I was the biggest shit heel this side of the Rockies.

"But you left out the most important thing," she went on. "You won. Before you met me, you lost all the time, and then I came into your life, and you won. And not just a couple hundred dollars, either. We're talking thousands, so far. How can you argue with that?"

"I can't."

"I'm very disappointed in you, James. You broke Rule Number Two. You lied to me."

"Well, in my own defense," I tried to explain, "I started checking up on you before you helped me win. I was just trying to protect myself. You know, from getting taken for a ride."

Amaris bristled. "And how was I going to do that? I hadn't even asked for any money yet."

"I thought maybe you were stringing me along. Setting me up for a big score."

"In what way?"

"I don't know," I said, examining a crumb left on the table by a previous occupant. The crumb and I had a lot in common. "I wasn't thinking clearly."

"That's the understatement of all time. So, after you won, why did you still feel the need for this confrontation?"

I shrugged, "I guess I felt betrayed."

"Let's get one thing straight," she said, poking me in the chest with a long smiley-face fingernail. "If anyone should feel betrayed, it's me. You got that?"

"Yes, ma'am." I hung my head. I've played the contrition card in my time, but this wasn't pretend.

"So," she asked, "what do we do now? Today's Wednesday. Your deadline's Friday. Do we move ahead or forget the whole thing? It's your call."

"No hard feelings?"

"Don't be an idiot. Of course I've got hard feelings. I'm only human. Well, mostly. But business is business. And the stars are extremely favorable for tomorrow evening."

I could feel myself getting pulled back into the game. But there was one thing I had to say. "I'm sorry, Amaris. I really am. You know the guy who stormed in here waving a rap sheet in your face? That was the old me. But from now on it's the new me." I swallowed, and suddenly my mind's eye was filled with the most distinct image of my mother I'd had in thirty years.

"James," Amaris said. "Thank you for everything, past, present, and future."

I smiled at her. She smiled back, her eyes clouding over. Then, she spread out some kind of astral chart and launched into a fifteen-minute dissertation. I hung on every word. When she was done, I didn't understand any more than when we started. Except that the stars were still favorable. But Amaris was clearly excited, and that was good enough for me.

It was time to call it a night. Despite my best efforts, I hadn't been able to fuck this up completely. Even better, we'd been at Denny's close to an hour, and hadn't seen a single waitress. Thank God, some things never change.

31

I had this fantasy. Because I hadn't heard from Poon in a while, I daydreamed that maybe he decided to drop my case. Or that, somehow, my file fell through the cracks. Or best of all, the bastard died of a massive heart attack. Jimmy Sr. used to tell me never to wish anybody dead. I'm not sure that applied to rogue IRS agents.

Unfortunately, my little delusion evaporated as soon as I got back to the condo. There, on the answering machine, was Poon's mocking voice, saying, "Hello, Jimmy. Stanford Poon here. Just a friendly reminder that your payment is due on Friday. Of course, if it's already in the mail, please disregard this notice."

The little prick sounded so fucking pleasant. And careful, too. Nothing on that tape could be construed as anything but a courtesy call from my affable taxman. Instantly, my fantasy morphed into another, darker, vision. In this one, I burst into his office, slam the cashier's check down on his desk, and, while he's examining it, shoot him between the eyes. If the Catholics are right, I'm going to hell.

It was late, but I decided to call Jenny. I needed to hear her voice. Joy answered instead. I was about to hang up, when she snapped, "What is it, Jimmy?"

"How'd you know it was me?"

"I just got caller ID. It helps screen out the pests." Pause. "You're lucky I picked up."

Ignoring her, I said, "Let me talk to Jenny."

I could hear Joy exhale on the other end. "Jimmy, it's after ten o'clock. Jenny's sleeping."

"I won't take long."

"Not a chance. She needs her rest. And while I'm on the subject, when Jenny's with me, she'll eat what I make her. When she's with you, you can feed her whatever the hell you like."

Jeez, I thought, I didn't even say anything to Jenny, and I'm still getting shit. But James, I told myself, it's the new you. Even though Joy'll never see it. "I didn't call to argue with you."

"That's a first," she said.

"Just do me one favor. Give her this message for me. Tell her I love her and that, whatever happens, I'll always be her Dad."

"Jesus, Jimmy, what do you want to do? Give her nightmares?"

"Just tell her. Please. It's important to me."

"What the devil have you gotten yourself into?" she asked. It sounded like an accusation.

"I'll let you know after Friday. Promise you'll do this one thing for me. I'll never ask for anything again."

"Okay, Jimmy. Since you've been so nice to my sister." Another pause. "There's nothing going on between you two, is there?"

I started to say, "Yeah, I'm boffing her every night. Twice on Sundays," but I just couldn't.

Joy didn't wait. "Well, it's none of my business."

"Yeah. Anyway, thanks. I owe you one."

"More than one," she said.

We hung up. Well, I thought, that went better than expected. I looked at the clock. The smart thing to do would be to try to get a good night's sleep. But I knew that would be impossible. The way my brain was leapfrogging from one feverish thought to the next, I'd be tossing and turning like a malaria victim.

Instead, I drove to the bar. Except for Bev and Mick and a couple of drunks, the place was a morgue. And I should know.

"Well, if it isn't Jimmy D," Bev said. "Are you rich yet?"

"This close," I said, indicating a sliver of space between my thumb and forefinger.

"Your timing's good, for once. I was just about to close up." She removed her apron in one fluid motion, throwing it on the counter next to the cash register. "Now it's your turn."

She and Mick took off, leaving me with the drunks. I poured them each a farewell beverage.

"On the house," I told them.

"Thanks, Jimmy," the older one mumbled. "You're the best."

Yeah, I thought. A week from now, you won't even remember my name. I called a cab and sent them on their way. Then, like I'd done a thousand times before, I turned my attention to all the little tasks that constituted my closing routine. Wash the glasses, wipe down the bar, turn off the appliances, stick the cash in the safe, and a dozen others too mundane to mention. I was in no particular hurry; I wanted to soak it all in, burn the images and the smells and the textures into my memory, so I could always transport myself back to this spot simply by shutting my eyes. When I completed my chores, I poured myself a beer, lit up a cigarette, sat down at the bar, and slowly scanned the room, seeing it as if for the first time.

"Well, Pop," I said, "if you can hear me, I could use a little help. Maybe you can put in a good word for me. If not, I'll understand. Lord knows, I don't deserve it. Besides, you probably have more important things to do." If I was expecting some kind of sign, a clap of thunder or a flickering of lights, it never came.

Instead, a raspy voice said, "Who ya talkin' to, Jimmy?"

You think I'd be used to it by now. I wheeled around, my heart clawing its way out of my chest, and blared, "Pete, I'm gonna have to strangle you!"

"Sorry, Jimmy. I forget, sometimes."

I took a breath. "Don't worry about it. Lately, yelling at you is the only exercise I get."

When he grinned, I noticed a missing front tooth. Just like Jenny. Except I don't think the Tooth Fairy visits the homeless.

"What happened here?" I asked, pointing to his mouth.

"Oh, that," he said. "Somebody gave me one of those foreign beers that doesn't have a twisty cap. I tried to open it with my teeth. It wasn't a very good idea."

"Ouch," I said, wincing.

"It's not that big a deal."

Anxious to change the subject, I said, "I'm glad you stopped by."

"Really?" he asked. "I don't hear that very much."

"I want to thank you for recommending that Dice Angel."

"Who?" Pete looked confused. He wasn't having one of his better days.

I said, "You know, Amaris. The Dice Angel. The woman who brings you luck at craps."

Suddenly, a glimmer of recognition blipped through his brain. "Oh, right, right, right. She's good, huh?"

"I think so. I'll find out for sure tomorrow night."

"That's great, Jimmy. I hope you win a lot of money."

"Listen, Pete, if for some reason it doesn't work out and I wind up losing this place, I want you to call me." I wrote my home number down on a to-go menu. It was probably a big mistake, but I couldn't leave this guy hanging. "Will you do that?"

"Sure. How come?"

"So I can let you know where I land. Maybe you can still come around."

I think Pete was touched. In more ways than one. He tried to give me a hug, but I deftly sidestepped him, offering my hand instead. It would be easier to wash.

"I'm gonna miss you, Jimmy," he said.

"Don't say that. I'll still be around."

His look gave me chills. "Thanks for being my friend."

When Pete finally hit the road, it was after one o'clock. Too late to go home. Retreating to my office, I wrestled the air mattress out of the corner, topping it off with a couple of extra breaths. Just like old times. So why, I asked myself, did it feel like the last time?

32

According to Amaris, pyramids have special properties. "Their hidden mathematics," she told me, "have the ability to convert universal biocosmic energy into magnetic, electrostatic, and gravitational forces and effects." As usual, I had no idea what she was talking about. I'm not sure Einstein would have understood her. All I knew was that we were making our final play at Luxor, the thirty-story glass pyramid at the south end of the Strip.

"The vibration is very powerful," she assured me. "And that beam shooting out from the top? It's a healing light. The brightest in the world. Did you know the astronauts can see it from space?"

"I hope the astronauts have better things to do."

That's when she called me a fuddy-duddy and said I'd best shape up before later that night.

Don't get me wrong. I like Luxor as much as the next guy. It's good cheesy fun. Where else can you stumble around in an exact replica of Pharaoh's tomb, ride an elevator sideways, listen to talking animatronic camels, and watch a remote-control King Tut sing "Walk Like an Egyptian"?

Of course, like most things in Las Vegas, there's a dark side. Roughly once a year, some poor slob takes a header off the inside top-floor balcony. It's easy to do. The railing only comes up about waist high and there's nobody to stop you if you're so inclined. Local legend has it that one guy went splat in the middle of a blackjack table and that, without missing a beat, the dealer asked, "Insurance, anyone?"

In any event, Luxor was the chosen site for Jimmy D's last stand. At 7:05, having showered, shaved, and shat, I pointed the Mazda in the direction of the giant pyramid. As it had been doing lately, the car made a disturbing clunking noise when I shifted into reverse. If by some miracle I won enough money, I'd leave that piece of crap in the parking garage with the engine running and a sign that read, "Free to Good Home."

In the old days, which in Vegas means ten years ago, the Strip was only busy on weekends. Now, it's bumper to bumper all the fucking time. Getting from point A to point B is like driving in a video game, with every manner of vehicle shooting out from well-concealed driveways, while wave after wave of pedestrians clog the streets like human sludge. For some reason, the element of make-believe, not to mention all the free booze, clouds their minds and they're drawn to cars like bugs to a zapper. By now, road-kill tourists are such a non-story, they bury it on page eighteen of our local rag, if they bother to run it at all.

As I headed south on the Strip past Excalibur (known around here as the "world's largest Motel 6"), I managed to avoid doing any serious damage to the wandering herds of cash cows. Perhaps there was a commendation in my future from the Convention and Visitors Authority. For a while, I got stuck behind a tanker truck bearing the warning, "Inedible Food. Unfit for Human Consumption." Hmm, I mused, they must be delivering to the Circus Circus buffet.

My under-inflated tires made a pathetic squealing sound as I pulled into Luxor's parking garage. I parked on the first floor, taking the steps two at a time up to the walkway on Casino Level. As I entered the joint, I passed a repulsive gnome of a man with a stunning blonde on his arm. You see this so often in Vegas, it's almost a cliché. The men always wear the same shit-eating smirk, as if to say, "Look at me. Ain't I something?" Meanwhile, everybody else is thinking the same thing: "I wonder how much she costs?"

Snaking my way through the crowded casino, I could over-hear fragments of conversation all around me. "I don't know how people can live here," a middle-aged woman was telling her friend. "They'd be broke all the time."

An older lady was saying, "Take my advice, Madge, never come to Las Vegas in the summer. It's like a blast furnace."

A teenage boy with a pierced eyebrow said to his buddy, "Shit, I still don't know how they figured out it was a fake ID."

A white-haired gentleman was explaining to a younger man, "Things were better in the old days. They really knew how to treat you back then. These punks today don't know the first thing about customer service."

From time to time, a shrill scream would rise above the casino buzz, indicating that some lucky person had just won money. More often than not, it makes no difference whether the amount is $50 or $50,000; the decibel levels are roughly the same. You can almost see the few locals in the casino shaking their heads and muttering, "Tourists." Those of us who live here are a pretty jaded bunch. It's hard for us to remember that many of our visitors have scrimped and saved their entire lives for that three-day dream vacation to the Entertainment Capital of the World.

Eventually, I arrived at the Nile Deli, our pre-arranged ren-dezvous point, to wait for Amaris. That's one of the problems with these themed resorts; the theme doesn't always work. I mean, the ancient Egyptians weren't exactly known for making a killer pas-trami sandwich.

After weeks of worry and headaches and aggravation, I was surprised to find myself unnaturally calm. One way or the other, it would all be over tonight. In a few hours, I'd know how it was going to end.

To kill time, I watched a frail elderly woman feed dollars into a Megabucks machine. The jackpot was a little over seventeen mil-lion, payable over twenty years. This poor lady looked like she didn't have twenty weeks. If she won, she'd be better off taking the lump sum. Each time she dropped a token into the slot, it made a greedy gulping sound. That's when I realized she was only play-ing two coins at a time. To hit the jackpot, you have to play three. It's the difference between winning seventeen mil and ten grand.

Normally, I wouldn't say anything. But she looked like such a sweet person, probably somebody's grandmother, and I needed all the good will I could muster. So I decided to break one of my cardinal rules.

"Excuse me," I said, giving her what I hoped was a winning smile. "I don't mean to interrupt, but I couldn't help noticing you're only putting in two coins. You'll have to play three if you want to be Nevada's newest millionaire."

"Young man," she said, "you play your money and I'll play mine."

Serves me right, I thought. "Best of luck, ma'am," I told her, slinking back to my previous spot. At least she called me "young man."

Amaris was waiting for me. At least, it sounded like Amaris.

"Hello, James," she said cheerily.

The person standing before me could have been a complete stranger. Gone were the layers of make-up, the loopy clothes, and the extraterrestrial perm. In their place was a handsome older woman, looking quite elegant in a black designer gown, understated pearl necklace, and matching earrings. She could have been right at home on the red carpet of the Oscars, preparing to receive her lifetime achievement award. I just stood there for a few moments with my mouth open.

"You like?" she asked, doing a little pirouette.

"Damn," I stammered. "What happened to you? I mean, you look great."

Amaris seemed pleased. "I'm in disguise," she said mysteriously.

"You should do it more often."

Whispering in my ear, she confided, "There was a slight … incident … here a number of months back. I didn't want to take any chances." Before I could press her for details, she asked, "So, James, are you ready to go to work?"

At this, my stomach tightened. "Absolutely," I said, trying to sound confident. Then I heard myself ask, "How's the vibe tonight?"

Her eyes lit up. "James, that's an excellent question. As a matter of fact, it couldn't be better. Now listen carefully. It's not going to be like last time, when you parlayed eleven and went home. Then, it was every man for himself. Tonight, it's all about team-work. We're looking for a hot table, specifically one shooter who's on fire. All he or she needs to do is hold the dice for twenty min-utes and you've got your bar back."

"Sounds good to me," I said shakily. "Any final words of wis-dom?"

"Just this. Trust the universe."

"Not a problem."

"And no matter what happens, count your blessings."

That one, I wasn't so sure about.

33

There were seven dice tables in the pit area, all of them open. As before, Amaris circled the pit like a wolf, scanning for God knows what kind of clues, sensory or otherwise. I was growing impatient when she finally pointed to a particular table and said in a low voice, "This one."

I gulped. It all seemed perfectly ordinary to me. "Are you sure?"

Her eyes glowed in the casino lights. "The signs are all positive."

"You sound like my Magic Eight-Ball," I said, trying for a little joke.

"That's where I get all my best material," she said, smiling. Then she added, "Now quit stalling."

"Don't go anywhere," I begged, but she'd already zoned out.

As soon as there was a break in the action, I took a deep breath and squeezed into a spot near the middle of the table, dropping fifty $100 bills on the layout. The dealer, a stout man with a pockmarked complexion and a unibrow, asked, "Any green?"

"All black," I told him.

He raised his caterpillar eyebrow and pushed a disturbingly small stack of chips my way. Glancing around, I quickly sized up the other players. They were such a diverse group, they reminded me of a low-rent version of the U. N. General Assembly.

The kid next to me couldn't have been more than twenty-one

or twenty-two, and he was betting $500 chips. This, too, is a common Vegas occurrence. I'd love to know where these boys get the money. The chips were royal blue and featured the likeness of a Pharaoh called the Sun King, a guy who would have felt right at home in our little desert community.

"How's it going?" I asked the kid. He was sporting shades and a Yankees cap.

"Up and down," he said.

"Cocktails!" a bubbly little server chirped. Her low-cut tunic showed off her unnaturally large breasts to full effect.

Jiggling the ice in his empty glass, my young neighbor said, "Bring me another zombie, and keep 'em coming until I am one." To assure friendly continuous service, he laid a $25 toke on her tray, eliciting a charming smile and a warm "Thank you, sir."

"Nothing wrong with that," the kid said to me, indicating our server.

"Nothing at all," I agreed. When I caught her eye, I said, "I'd like a club soda."

"Lime?" she asked sweetly.

"Sure, what the hell. Live dangerously, that's my motto."

Just then, the stickman yelled, "New shooter! Comin' out!"

I plopped a chip on the pass line and tried to think happy thoughts. The shooter was a lanky sunburned man in a brocade shirt and Stetson hat. He took a swig from a long-neck bottle of Coors, meticulously selected two dice, and pitched them in a smooth backhand motion toward the far end of the table.

"Baby needs a pair of shoes!" he shouted, the hokiest expression in the book. Other than in the movies, I'd never heard anyone actually say it before. And yet, the rest of the players laughed appreciatively.

"Easy eight, the point is!" said the stickman.

"Good number! Good number!" cheered a man in a white turban.

The casino offered five times odds, so I placed five more blacks behind my original bet. The rest of my chips fit easily into the palm of my hand, where I nervously rubbed them together.

"Bets down," the stickman said.

Tex took another pull off his beer and tossed the dice.

"Eight! Winner, easy eight, it came right back," the stickman announced to the approval of the crowd.

"We got us a shooter!" whooped a good old boy with a ZZ Top beard.

"Helluva start," I told my young friend.

"Damn straight," he agreed.

As the dealer paid me $700, I spun around to check on Amaris. She was there in body only.

Still, she deserved a compliment. "Nice work," I said, hoping she could hear me. I think I detected the hint of a smile.

The voice of the stickman refocused my attention. "Same shooter! Working bets have action."

I bumped my pass line bet up to $200 and watched Tex throw a seven. The players roared with delight. They were really getting worked up now.

"Seven! Winner seven! Pay the line."

"Get 'em out of your system!" squealed a blowzy redhead.

I increased my flat bet to $300. Just before Tex rolled again, an insistent voice whispered, "Bet the seven." If it was Amaris, she was communicating via ESP. But it seemed more like a hunch. Although it's one of the worst bets in the game, I flipped a $100 chip toward the dealer and said, "Big Red."

Son-of-a bitch if the cowboy didn't pull another seven out of his ass.

"Front-line winner," the stickman proclaimed. With my proposition bet, I was another $700 to the good.

My neighbor gave me a high-five and said excitedly, "Dude, I *love* this fuckin' game!"

As the Texan prepared for his next roll, a cute little gal in matching shirt and hat grabbed him by the arm and said, "Wes, it's time to go eat. Our reservation's for eight."

With a look of absolute irritation, he yanked his arm away and said, "Not now, darlin'! Can't you see I'm on a little ol' hot streak?"

"But I'm hungry," she pouted.

"Fuck this shit," muttered my friend. "She's killing our momentum."

"I know," I said glumly.

"Leave him alone!" ZZ Top bellowed.

The crowd chimed in. "Let him roll!" We were so boisterous, the pit boss peered up from his papers and delivered a withering stare.

"Settle down, y'all," Wes told us. Turning back to his girl, he said, "Honey, you go get us our table, and I'll be there shortly." Handing her a chip, he added, "In the meantime, order yourself a bottle of that Dom Perignon you like so much."

As she examined the chip, her face broke into a Texas-sized grin. "All right," she said. "But if you keep this up, I'm goin' shoppin'."

"Whatever makes you happy," he drawled.

We all watched her sashay across the floor. When she had wiggled out of sight, Wes announced, "Sorry about that, fellers."

"Okay," the stickman said, "same shooter. Crap, eleven, any seven."

Wes heaved the dice.

"Ten. Hard ten. The number's ten," the stickman informed us.

I stuck $1,500 in back of my original bet and another $100 on the come.

"Five on the hop," my young friend said, plunking a blue chip on the table. It rolled a short distance before coming to rest directly in front of me. I took that to be some sort of sign.

"Same here," I instructed the dealer, tossing a black on the layout. If the very next roll came up five, it paid 15 to 1, a bad proposition if there ever was one. I looked at the kid and shrugged. "What the fuck, right?"

"If it hits, it's a good bet," he said, grinning like a madman.

"Five hopping," the dealer acknowledged. "Five on the hops-i-chord!"

The stickman said, "Watch your hands, dice are moving." One of them stopped on two. The other spun around and around like a top for what seemed like an hour. The air crackled with anticipation. We all leaned in breathlessly to see how it would land.

"Five!" the stickman called, and the kid gave me a hug. He was my newest best friend in all the world. Hell, he was like a brother to me. And the rest of the players were family, too. They were the finest group of people I'd ever known.

The stickman reminded us, "The number's still ten." I now

had a bet on the five from the come line. I put out another black on the come.

Wes rolled a four. The dealer moved my come bet to four on the layout, and I added $500 odds, plus another chip on the come.

"If you can roll a four, you can roll a ten!" I laughed. The shooter gave me a wink and said, "Just watch me, son."

Wes threw a six. Same routine as before.

Wes threw another six.

"Off and on," the dealer said, handing me the profit.

Wes rolled an eight. More of the same.

"Make the stinkin' point!" the redhead shrieked.

Wes was only too happy to oblige.

"Ten! Front-line winner!" The table went apeshit. Whooping and hollering and backslapping all around. We were getting rich together. All except a rumpled sad little man who had been playing the don'ts, which is kind of like betting the stock market to crash. While we celebrated, he shook his head and trudged slowly away.

Same shooter. My previous bets were still up. I increased my line bet to $500 and put another chip on crap/eleven for insurance.

"Gimme some of that action," Wes said, and threw the dice.

"Yo-'leven!" the stickman bellowed.

"Hot damn!" Wes exclaimed.

I was in total agreement. "In-fucking-credible!"

The dealer paid me $500 for my line bet, plus another $700 for the yo. I parlayed the pass line, making it $1,000.

Wes rolled a four for the new point.

"Four, the point is four!" the stickman said. "Fo' to go!"

I stuck five grand odds in back of my flat bet, turning to glance at Amaris for reassurance. None came. Her eyes were rolled back in her head like the shark in *Jaws*. Wherever she was, I prayed she could keep this up. I prayed for myself, as well. I was practically all in. My heart was doing two hundred miles per hour with no pit stop in sight.

Wes rolled an eight, and I pressed.

Wes rolled a six, and I pressed.

"Your club soda," my server said.

Handing her a black chip, I told her, "Go back, dump this glass out and fill it with your best Irish whiskey."

"My pleasure, sir!" she said, beaming.

Wes rolled a hard four! The table erupted like the volcano at the Mirage. We made so much noise, the players in the immediate vicinity stopped to see what the hell was going on. So did the pit boss, a chinless man with skin the color of bad cottage cheese, taking in the whole scene with utter scorn.

"Four, winner four the hard way," the stickman said. "Little Joe from Kokomo!"

Little Joe paid a little over $11,000 on my front-line action. The rail in front of me was filling up with blue and black chips, but I didn't dare count them. That's the gospel according to Kenny Rogers.

My new kid brother jumped up and down so high, his cap fell off. "Pinch me, I'm dreaming!" he sang.

One man's dream is another man's nightmare. The pit boss slithered over to the box man and whispered something in his ear. In short order, the son-of-a-bitch was inspecting the dice, holding each one up to the light, turning his hand at different angles, squinting like a wholesale jeweler.

"New dice!" he ordered.

The players exploded in a chorus of boos.

"These guys kill me," I told the kid. "They're more superstitious than we are."

"What a prick," he said.

In my head, I heard Amaris say, "It doesn't matter."

"Fuck 'em," I said, and bumped my pass line bet to $2,000. The kid looked at me like I was nuts, but followed my lead.

The pit boss should have stuck with the old dice. Because Wes was still hotter than Vegas in July. Five minutes later, the boss made another uninvited appearance. Only this time, he changed the whole crew. The boos and catcalls were rowdier than ever. For a moment, I thought he might call security.

"Can you believe this cocksucker?" I asked the kid out of the side of my mouth.

"I'm writing a nasty letter."

"Leave it to management to blame the dealers."

"It's Vegas, man," he said with a look of resignation.

"I feel bad for our crew. Let's toke 'em."

"Good idea."

The kid and I each lobbed a $500 chip onto the felt. "Nice going, you guys!" I called out.

"Here, here!" Wes agreed, and in no time at all, everybody was tossing chips and clapping their hands wildly. In total, there must have been $2,500 in tokes on the table. While the dealers and stickman bowed and declared their undying gratitude, the pit boss's face was turning a more sickly shade of yellow.

The new crew, when they arrived, looked older and meaner. The A-team. After they'd taken up their positions, I informed them, "Stick with us and we'll show you a good time." I may as well have been speaking Swahili. Not a nod, not a smile, not a glimmer of recognition. Just the dark vacant stares of a nest of king cobras.

But the new crew could perform no snake magic this night. Our collective mojo was too powerful. The Texan still held the dice, and he continued to hold them for I don't know how long. For the first time in my life, I was so in the moment, I lost track of everything but those red numbered cubes. Somewhere in the back of my mind, I knew I must have been approaching my goal. But I didn't want to break the spell.

A loud commotion shattered it for me. Like a house of cards, it all came crashing down when I heard a gruff no-nonsense voice bark, "Ma'am, I'm not going to say it again. You're going to have to leave the premises. Now!"

Whirling around so fast I nearly gave myself whiplash, I saw the source of the voice: a bloated casino executive in a blue pinstripe suit. To my astonishment, he was speaking to Amaris.

"Why?" she asked, stamping her foot. "I wasn't doing anything. I have just as much right to be here as you do."

The fat man made a subtle head gesture and, without warning, two beefy security guards were all over Amaris, one on each side, locking up her arms and dragging her toward the exit, her high heels leaving little ragged trails on the carpet. To her credit, she didn't go without a fight, wriggling and kicking and clawing every step of the way. All eyes in the casino were riveted on the bizarre scene: another Vegas story to entertain the folks back home.

"You can't do this to me!" Amaris screamed. "You'll pay for this! You're all in karmic debt!"

Well, that ought to scare 'em, I thought. I didn't know whether to try to help or hang on to my precious spot. I used the delay to take a quick assessment of my financial situation. I had roughly $40,000 in the rail and another $15,000 on the table. If I cashed out now, I'd be $12,000 short, taking Amaris' commission into account. Just three more numbers and I'd be over the top.

As Amaris faded from sight, I heard her yell, "Take him down, take him down!" That's when it hit me like a shotgun blast. Rule Number One: "You must never gamble without me." But what choice did I have? It's not like Poon was going to settle for anything less than the full amount. Besides, it wasn't just about the money anymore. This was about redemption.

"Forgive me," I thought, and I didn't know if I was talking to Amaris or myself or whoever.

"What the hell was that all about?" the kid asked. I just shook my head.

"All right," the stickman said sourly. "Show's over. Same shooter. Point's still nine."

I crossed my fingers and watched as Wes let the dice fly.

34

Afterwards, I found Amaris sitting on the hood of my car, her arms wrapped around her drawn-up legs. From the rivulets of mascara streaking down her cheeks, I could tell she'd been crying. The scuffle had ripped a strap off her designer gown and she was missing the heel of her right shoe.

"I was worried about you," I said. "Are you okay?"

Slowly, her eyes panned up to meet mine. After a long pause, she sighed, "I am so sorry." Then, the words came rushing out in a torrent. "I thought they might recognize me but the signs were so perfect and I knew it was a chance we'd have to take but I never meant for this to happen the way it did and I let you down and—"

"Amaris," I tried to interrupt, but she kept right on going.

"—now you'll lose the bar and it's all my fault and why did I ever think I could make this work again, and—"

"Amaris!" I said more forcefully, clapping my hands six inches from her face. The noise reverberated through the parking garage like a gunshot.

She stopped in mid-babble. "What?" she asked, really focusing on me for the first time. Then she was off and running again. "Honestly, James, was that really necessary? I deserve to be treated with a little respect, you know, like a human being, not some animal you can just scare any time you feel like; I mean, I'm feeling delicate enough right now, thank you, without you wandering over here and—"

"Oh, for God's sake!" I howled in exasperation. "I won, Amaris, I won. So stop pissing and moaning."

I could see the recognition flicker across her face like a sunrise, illuminating each feature before taking up residence in her eyes.

She blinked once. "You won?"

"Yeah."

"How can that be?"

"Your guess is as good as mine. All I know is, sixty thousand in hundreds feels like a brick in my pocket."

"You won," she repeated, and this time a smile stretched from ear to ear. "Well, of course you did. How can a couple of corporate fascists hope to compete with a benevolent universe?"

"That," I assured her, "is a very good question. Hey, I got something for you." I reached into my other pocket and pulled out a wad of bills the size of a baseball, bound together by an oversized rubber band. "Here, catch," I said. She deftly snatched it with one hand, her eyes growing wide. "Fifteen large," I told her. "Go ahead, count it."

Still staring at the money, Amaris shook her head. "I trust you, James. You know that."

Both of us looked at the roll appreciatively. Finally, she said, "So, what happened after I left?"

"More of the same. That Texas son-of-a-gun kept right on making numbers. Still is, for all I know. Probably owns the goddamned Sphinx by now. As soon as I made my nut, I scooped up the money and got the hell out of there. No use getting greedy, right?"

"That's a very enlightened attitude."

"Want to hear the funniest part?"

"Sure."

"As I was cashing out, that rat-bastard pit boss asked if he could comp my room, food, and drinks. You know, anything to keep me around so they could take another shot at me. Just like a real high roller."

"What did you say?" Amaris asked.

"I told him I was staying at Bellagio."

She chuckled and asked, "Then what happened?"

"I wandered around the casino, looking for you. The whole time, I kept checking to make sure I wasn't being tailed. All I need is for somebody to follow me out to the car and bop me over the head. Or worse."

"You could have had a security escort," she said. "Like I did."

"I'll pass, thanks. I don't trust those guys, either. So tell me, what did you do to deserve the red-carpet treatment back there?"

"A couple of months ago," she explained, "I was here with another client. He won, too. Not as much as you, but a substantial amount. It got their attention. They couldn't prove anything, but when did that ever matter? Apparently, they've been circulating my picture, and word got around. I'm in the Griffin book now."

I whistled in admiration. "Persona non grata, huh? Very impressive."

"They think I'm some sort of cheater. It's an honor, really."

"I wonder how they recognized you."

"It's those eye-in-the-sky people. That's all they do. I hear they can zoom in and read the serial numbers off a hundred dollar bill. I'm afraid my tattoo might have given me away." She pointed to a tiny half-moon on her left shoulder.

"What'll you do now?"

Sliding off the hood of my car, she said, "I don't know. Maybe live it up a little. I hear Monte Carlo is lovely this time of year. Thanks to you, I have traveling money."

"I didn't do anything. All I did was show up."

"Well," she said, "sometimes that's enough."

Walking over to her, I cupped her chin in my hand and kissed her tenderly. She tasted like Juicy Fruit.

"See!" she said. "You fell in love with me. I knew you would."

My face flushed red. "Well, maybe a little."

"Don't get too attached," she warned. "You've got a bar to run."

35

I sang in the car on the way back to Jimmy D's. "Money, that's what I want!" and "Money for nothin' and your chicks for free!" and, of course, "We're in the money, we're in the money ..." I didn't know the rest of the words, so I finished up with a grating off-key "dee-dee-da-dee-da-dee-da-dee-da-dee-dee!" The windows were down and the night air was just cool enough to be refreshing. Each time I stopped for a light, people in the car next to me would laugh or point or shake their heads. I couldn't care less. They didn't have $60,000 in their pockets and a future stretching before them like a freshly paved highway.

I slid through the front door a la Tom Cruise in *Risky Business*. The bar was uncharacteristically busy for 10:30 on a Thursday night. Maybe the word had leaked out that this was the end of the line for the venerable Vegas watering hole. Too bad I couldn't milk that a while longer, the way Michael Jordan did with his "retirements."

Positioning myself in the center of the room, I shouted, "Excuse me, ladies and gentlemen, but I have an announcement to make!" Instantly, all conversation stopped. "Thank you," I continued. "It's nice to see so many old friends here tonight. I just want to say that tomorrow, it will be business as usual at Jimmy D's." A cheer rose up from the crowd. Never being one to leave well enough alone, I had to add, "And tonight, the drinks are on me."

More cheering, even from the few patrons who had no idea what was going on. When I could make my way over to Bev and Mick, I said in a low voice, "Hide the good stuff."

Bev asked, "So how'd you do it, Jimmy?"

Digging into my pocket, I extracted the thick packet of hundreds and slammed it onto the bar.

"Jesus, Mary, and Joseph!" Bev exclaimed, crossing herself.

Mick just gaped at the bills, a comical expression on his weather-beaten face.

With forced nonchalance, I said, "Let's just say I had an unusually lucky night at the tables." Winking at Bev, I added, "Might have been the St. Christopher's medal."

"Praise the Lord," she said. Glancing around furtively, she whispered, "You'd better put that money away, before somebody gets a bright idea."

"Good thinking." I slipped the roll back into my pocket. Giving Bev a swift peck on the cheek, I headed for my office, saying, "Keep these folks entertained. I have to make a phone call."

It had occurred to me that I'd better contact Poon and tell him to call off his dogs. Even though he wouldn't be working at this hour, I could leave a message on voicemail. To my surprise, he answered the phone.

"You're working late," I said, when I realized he wasn't a recording. "Trying to figure out how to put more widows and orphans on the street?"

"Just saloon owners," he said, recognizing my voice. "If it isn't the living legend, Jimmy D. I had a hunch I might be hearing from you."

"Yeah, why's that?"

"You know, the usual. Begging and pleading for an extension. They all do it. But I must warn you, it won't help. At this stage, not even the Commissioner himself can intervene. Not that he would, you understand."

Time to drop the bombshell, I thought. Damn, this was sweet. "Well," I said, "that won't be necessary."

"Really. How so?"

"I've got the money."

Long pause.

"Did you hear me?" I asked. "I said, 'I've got the money.'"

"Oh," he said. It came out in a short burst, as if he'd been kicked in the solar plexus. Rallying quickly, he continued, "I mean, that's wonderful, Jimmy. Very good news, indeed." I could tell he was choosing his words carefully. No doubt, all calls in and out of that building were taped to better serve me. "You've got the entire amount, I trust?" he asked.

"Every last dime. Why don't I stop by tomorrow morning and we'll settle up. How's eleven o'clock sound?"

He made a big deal out of checking his schedule. "Eleven, eleven," he said. "I'm sorry, I have an appointment at eleven. How about two? I'm free then."

"Sure. I don't mind hanging onto my dough a while longer."

"Okay, two it is." He couldn't even fake enthusiasm.

"Looking forward to it," I told him. "I can't wait to see your nose."

36

On Friday morning, I slept in until 8:30, ate a leisurely break-fast of toast and coffee, then smoked one final cigarette before flush-ing the rest down the toilet. I couldn't remember the last time I felt so good. I was getting my life back. And this time, I was going to appreciate it.

It was a clear crisp winter's day. Heading to Jimmy D's to re-trieve the cash from the safe, I played drums on the dashboard while the classic-rock station blasted Zeppelin's "Whole Lotta Love."

Even the news couldn't dampen my mood. It was the usual shit. A hostage situation on the west side. A talking head assuring us that Vegas had enough water to last until 2026. (Then what? Would we all be showering in champagne?) And a late-breaking story: A teenage boy had plowed through a school crosswalk, kill-ing the guard and sending three fourth-graders to the hospital. A damned shame. Now that I'm older, I don't think anybody should be allowed to drive until they're thirty.

"Where've you been?" Bev asked as soon as I walked through the door. "I've been trying to reach you for the last half hour."

My stomach lurched. "Why? Was there another break-in?"

"No, your money's still here."

"That's a relief. What's up?"

"Sarah called. You can reach her at this number. She says it's urgent." She gave me the piece of scratch paper.

"Did she say why?"

"No. Just call."

"How'd she sound?"

"Bad."

I hurried to my office and punched in the number. The phone rang seven, eight, nine times. While I waited, I tucked the receiver under my chin and opened the safe. The money was right where I left it. I stuffed the bills into my pocket just as somebody picked up the phone.

"Hello," a strange male voice answered.

"Is Sarah there?" I asked nervously.

"I don't know." I heard him shout, "Is somebody named Sarah expecting a phone call?" After a few seconds, he came back on the line. "She's on her way."

At last, Sarah asked, "Jimmy?" The way she said my name, I could tell it was trouble.

"It's me."

"Oh, thank God," she said, bursting into tears. "It's Rachel … she's had a relapse … I called the ambulance and they took her to the hospital … It's not good, Jimmy … I think I'm going to lose her …"

"Sarah, slow down," I said. "What hospital are you at?"

"Desert Sun."

"What floor?"

"I don't know," she said between sobs. "Critical Care."

"I'll be there in fifteen minutes."

I ran every red light from the bar to Desert Sun Hospital, the giant medical complex on Eastern Avenue. Parking in a tow-away zone, I sprinted toward the entrance, stopping just long enough for the big electric double doors to swing open.

"Come on, come on," I ordered them, as if that would help speed things up. Flying through the lobby, I asked the elderly volunteer at the reception desk, "Where's Critical Care?"

"Third floor," she said. "But you'll have to register …"

Too late. I was already past her, finding the elevator, prodding the button repeatedly, not getting the desired response, finally racing up the stairs to the third floor.

"Critical Care!" I yelled at the first nurse I saw.

"The end of the hallway," she said, pointing. "But you'll need to ..."

I wasn't interested. I burst into the waiting room directly outside the locked door to Critical Care. That's where I found Sarah, slumped on an uncomfortable-looking vinyl couch, weeping silently into a Kleenex.

The woman sitting next to her could tell I meant business. She gathered up her knitting and moved to a chair on the other side of the room.

Lowering myself onto the couch beside Sarah, I wrapped her in my arms and let her cry. At last, in a faint voice she said, "Jimmy, I need your help."

"I'm right here."

"They're moving Rachel to County."

"What?" I asked. I couldn't have heard her right.

She said it again.

"Why the hell would they do something like that?"

She looked at me, her lower lip trembling. "I have no health insurance. Owen wasn't paying the premiums."

"Oh, for God's sake." Then a thought occurred to me. "What about life insurance? Don't you have a big check coming?"

She started crying again, big racking sobs that shook her whole body. "He didn't pay that either. I just found out." She looked at me. " How could he do something like this to his family, to his sick daughter?"

"I don't know," I whispered. I wanted to kill the son-of-a-bitch all over again.

"Jimmy," she pleaded, "don't let them take my Rachel. She's in a coma; they want to do surgery. It doesn't make sense. I just know if she goes to County, she'll die there."

"Who's in charge here?"

"I talked to a woman named Mrs. Burke in the finance office."

"Stay put," I told Sarah, squeezing her hand. It felt small and vulnerable. "I'll handle this. And whatever you do, don't let them move Rachel."

Mrs. Burke was a skinny hatchet-faced woman of about fifty-five. When I stormed into her cluttered office, she was talking to an old man with skin the texture of jerky, no doubt explaining why Medicare wouldn't begin to cover his expenses.

"Excuse me," I said to them. I stared daggers at the old man, who moved surprisingly fast for somebody his age.

Mrs. Burke looked at me with a mixture of fear and contempt. "You can't just barge in here like that!" she sputtered.

"I know, but this is an emergency."

"I'm calling security," she threatened.

I was about to give her the complete Jimmy D treatment when something in her eyes stopped me. They were mournful, as full of regret as a Dear John letter. This woman might have been good at her job, but the job was obviously killing her.

As she reached for the phone, I said quietly, "You don't have to do that. I'm sorry if I scared you. It's just that this is a life-and-death situation."

Her face softened a bit. "Aren't they all?"

"My name's Delaney," I said, extending my hand. She reached for it tentatively. "I represent Sarah Johnson."

Mrs. Burke pursed her lips. "The name doesn't ring a bell. You have to understand, we process a tremendous number of patients through this office."

I said, "Please check your records. Mrs. Johnson's daughter, Rachel, is scheduled to be transferred to County today."

She shuffled through a stack of computer printouts. Stopping to read a particular sheet of paper, she said, "Yes, I recall. Mrs. Johnson is uninsured. I'm simply following standard hospital procedure."

"Is there an alternative to moving Rachel?" I asked.

She shook her head, letting out a long sigh. "I don't see how."

"What if I switch Mrs. Johnson over to my policy?"

"It doesn't work that way," she said. "You don't know very much about insurance, do you?"

"It's not one of my strong suits," I said. "Okay, spell it out for me. What'll it take for Rachel to get the treatment she needs right here?"

Again, Mrs. Burke consulted her printout. "For somebody in her condition, with all of the necessary tests and procedures, we would need a credit card on account or a cash deposit in the amount of …" Squinting, she held the paper at arm's length, saying at last, "a minimum of fifty-thousand dollars."

"Fuck."

"I beg your pardon?"

"Just thinking out loud." Didn't it always come down to this? As if on cue, I felt the bankroll rubbing insistently against my thigh.

I must have been staring into space for quite some time. "Young man?" Mrs. Burke's voice interrupted my thoughts. "Are you all right?"

"Yeah. Fine. Never better." In a singular moment of clarity, I knew what had to be done. Before I could change my mind, I removed the bills from my pocket and placed them on Mrs. Burke's desk. The sight of all that money must have short-circuited her synapses.

"What's this?"

"Cash," I explained. "Sixty grand, to be exact. That oughta cover Rachel's expenses for a while, don't you think?"

Mrs. Burke gingerly poked at the stack with her index finger, the way you would a dead frog.

"Take it," I said. "It won't bite."

That's when she finally allowed herself a small tight smile.

"Do we have a deal, then?" I asked. It seemed like a long time before she replied.

"Why, yes," she said finally. "I believe we do."

"Good," I said. "Let's keep this just between us, okay?"

"Just between us," she repeated.

Then, in a rare display of business savvy, I added, "Don't forget my receipt."

Back in the waiting room, I said to Sarah, "It's all taken care of. Rachel can stay."

Throwing her arms around me, she asked, "But how, Jimmy?"

"You don't know this about me," I said, "but I can be pretty persuasive when I want to be."

37

Bridgett stuck her head into my office and said, "You've got a visitor. He's a cop."

I looked up from the inventory report and studied my new assistant manager. She was twenty-two, just out of college, tall and shapely, with olive skin. She did nothing for me.

"Thanks," I said.

Bridgett looked at me with a puzzled expression. "Are you in some kind of trouble?"

"Probably. Send him back."

A few seconds later, Wally filled the room. I stood to greet him. After the usual male bonding, he said, "How ya doin', Jimmy?"

"Better than nothing."

"I've been worried about you, but it looks like you landed on your feet. This place ain't bad."

Opening my bottom desk drawer, I produced a bottle of Midleton's and two shot glasses. "Join me?"

"What the hell."

I poured us a couple and Wally said, "Hang the rich."

"Hang 'em high," I agreed, and we drained our glasses.

"Damn, that's smooth," he said, licking his lips. Doing a quick three-sixty of my office, he said, "It's a helluva lot bigger than your old one."

"More to clean."

"So how's it working out for you?"

I paused. "Well, in some ways it's better. I mean, everything's new. I don't have to kick the ice machine or stick my head in the oven to light the pilot. Mr. O'Shaugnessy's an absentee owner; he spends most of his time back in Ireland. The guy's got more money than Trump, so the bar's just a tax write-off. He pretty much lets me run it however I want. And hire whoever I want. Bev finally retired, but I was able to take a few of my old employees with me."

"How about that old wino who used to hang around?"

"Pete? I gave him my forwarding address. We're a package deal."

"Sounds like one big happy family. So what's the problem?"

"Who said there's a problem?"

"Jimmy boy, I can tell just by looking at your ugly mug."

I shrugged. "The only problem is, the joint's not mine."

Wally said, "Yeah, there's that. I can't even drive past the old place without shedding a tear. Not literally, but you know what I'm talking about."

"I haven't been back since that fucking Poon boarded it up."

"When's the auction?"

I made a big deal out of checking the calendar, even though the date was permanently imprinted on my brain. "Why, it looks like tomorrow," I said, trying to sound casual.

"You gonna go?"

"Oh sure. And then I'm gonna track down all my old girlfriends and ask them why they broke up with me."

"I guess the answer's no."

"Wally, with an IQ like yours, you oughta make lieutenant any day now."

"Bite your tongue," he said, grimacing.

"Can't we talk about something more pleasant?"

"Sure. I hear Sarah's kid is doing great."

"Uh huh. They sent her home last week. She's not totally out of the woods, but the doctors are optimistic."

"That was a nice thing you did," Wally said.

"Don't tell anybody. I'd hate for the word to get out that Jimmy D's a sap."

"Saint's more like it."

I shook my head. "Saint my ass. It was the hardest decision I ever made."

"If it was easy," he said, "you wouldn't be a fuckin' saint."

"Well, I just kept picturing my daughter lying there. I'd hope somebody would do the same for me."

"It would be a better world, wouldn't it?" He smiled. "How is Jenny, by the way?"

"The best. Guess what I got her for her birthday?"

"What?"

"A beagle puppy. Cutest little bastard you ever saw. She named it Wally."

"You gotta be kidding me!" His eyes lit up. "I don't know whether to be flattered or insulted."

"It's your call. She said it's 'cause he eats raw meat."

"What a kid," he chuckled. "Tell me something. How'd you get Joy to go along with it?"

"I didn't. When Jenny came to visit, I sent her home with the dog. What's Joy gonna do, ship it back and break her little heart?"

"Probably not."

"But she did call and tear me a new one for over an hour. I actually laid the phone down and went to the bathroom and when I came back she was still yelling. Never missed a beat."

"So you pissed her off and made your kid happy. Sounds like a win-win to me."

"Here's the best part," I said. "At night, they keep the dog in the laundry room. In the morning, Joy says it looks like an explosion at the shit factory."

While Wally roared with laughter, I poured us another round.

"A toast," I said, lifting my glass. "To puppies."

"To puppies," he echoed. "The gift that keeps on giving."

38

The next day, Bridgett poked her head into my office again.

"You've got a visitor," she said. "Some lady named Sarah."

"Thanks," I said, feeling my day get suddenly brighter. "Ask her to come in."

Bridgett said, "You get a lot of company, don't you."

"Just lately."

Sarah looked great. I motioned for her to sit and she took the big comfortable chair in front of my desk.

"What a nice surprise."

She smiled and said, "I was in the neighborhood."

"Doing what?"

"Okay, so I wasn't in the neighborhood. I have some things to tell you and I thought it was better to do it in person."

I sat up a little straighter in my leather executive chair. It was a big improvement over my old thrift-store model, but I hated it just the same. "Before we get into all that, how's Rachel?"

"Better every day, knock on wood." She rapped her knuckles on the desktop. "The doctor says she's an amazing young lady; very resilient."

"That's the best news I've heard in a long time."

"Which reminds me," she said. "I owe you money." She reached in her purse and extracted a ten and a one, carefully laying them out in front of me.

I said, "I give up. What's this for?"

"The hospital sent me their final statement. You should see it; it's more than thirty pages, all itemized. Very impressive. Did you know they charge thirteen dollars for an aspirin?"

"No," I said, suddenly wishing the office had an emergency exit.

"Anyway, this money is the difference between what you paid and what they charged. There was some change also, but I think it's lost in the bottom of my purse."

I couldn't meet her eyes. Instead, I became overly interested in some pencil shavings on my desk.

"Say something," Sarah said.

I sighed. "You weren't supposed to know about it."

"Well, it wasn't tough to figure out. I mean, you're pretty convincing, but nobody's *that* good. Hospitals aren't in the business of giving things away. Even I know that."

"I thought it might slip through the cracks. You know, in all the excitement."

"Sorry. You're busted, mister." She was trying to be a hard-ass, but her eyes twinkled mischievously. She continued, "So that's my first order of business. To say 'thank you' for saving my daughter's life."

I mumbled, "Don't mention it." What the hell was I supposed to say at a time like this?

"Which brings me to my second order of business. You'll never guess what I did this morning."

"You got your nails done."

"Wrong. I decided to check out the auction at Jimmy D's."

If she didn't have my attention before, she had it now. "You're kidding."

She shook her head. "Nope. I've never been to an auction before. It's really interesting."

Despite my better judgment, I had to ask, "What happened?"

"There were a handful of serious bidders and a bunch of lookie-loos. The bidding got hot and heavy for a while. Finally, it went for something like three hundred sixty thousand. Is that a lot?"

"It's a steal," I said, suddenly depressed.

"Really? I'm glad to hear it," she said. For the life of me, I couldn't figure out why she was so happy.

"Who's the asshole that bought it?" I asked.

"You're looking at her."

I'm sure I sat there for a good minute, not comprehending. Something had gone horribly wrong with the circuit that connected my ears to my brain.

"Are you okay?" Sarah's voice came from the next galaxy. The sound of snapping fingers brought me back.

"Yeah," I rasped. "For a second, I thought you said you bought my old place. Pretty funny, huh?"

"That's exactly what I said, Jimmy." The expression on her face was deadly serious.

"Whoa," I said, holding up my hands. "If this is your idea of a joke—"

She cut me off. "It's no joke."

"Excuse me for asking then, but where in the hell did you get that kind of money?"

"Well, that's the unbelievable part," she said, as if the rest of our conversation had been normal. "Last week, two nice men from the government paid me a visit. I thought it had to do with some paperwork to close the books on Owen. But they had other things on their mind."

"What kind of things?"

"It seems they were terribly embarrassed about losing Owen like that. According to them, it almost never happens. And if the word gets out, there goes their precious witness-protection program. Can you imagine?"

"I'm starting to."

"So they gave me a check to keep me quiet. Hush money, I think it's called. Not by them, of course. They said it's more like an insurance settlement. Technically, I shouldn't even be talking to you."

"How much?" I asked.

"Five hundred thousand dollars."

"That'll buy a lot of insurance."

She laughed. "I know. I didn't tell them, but I would have taken less."

"Hush," I said, putting my finger to her lips.

"There's only one problem."

"Just one?"

"Yes. I don't know the first thing about running a saloon and supper club. Is there somebody you could recommend?"

I pretended to think for a moment. "As a matter of fact, I do know a guy. And it just so happens, he's not very happy in his present situation."

"Could you get in touch with him for me? I'd be very grateful."

"I'm sure I can negotiate on his behalf," I said. "But he doesn't work cheap. He'd have to be the general manager."

Sarah's eyes narrowed. "I was thinking more along the lines of partner."

"Partner," I repeated. "He'll like the sound of that."

"It's settled, then," she said, offering her hand. I took it and gave it a firm shake.

"Just one other thing," I said.

"Yes?"

"Do you think he could get a small advance? Say, around a thousand dollars?"

She said, "That's awfully brazen. Being new, and all."

Looking into those beautiful green eyes, I said, "He needs to get a watch out of hock."

About the Author

Brian Rouff has lived in Las Vegas since 1981, which makes him a long-timer by local standards. He is married with two grown daughters, and a new grandson. This is his first novel.

The author can be contacted at the following e-mail address: brouff55@aol.com

To order additional copies of this book, visit
www.greatstuff4gamblers.com

For information on Foundation Room Membership,
please call (702) 632-7614 or contact
the Foundation Room via email at
membership.foundationroom.lasvegas@postman.hob.com